Wild Words

Volume 3

Leitrim County Council Arts Office,
Aras an Chontae,
Carrick on Shannon,
Co. Leitrim,
Ireland.

+353 (71) 96 21694

www.leitrimarts.ie

ISBN: 9780957618930

Edited by Helen Carr

A collection of writing by young people produced as part of the Wild Words Children's Book Festival, Carrick on Shannon, Co. Leitrim.

Published by Leitrim County Council Arts Office

Contents

Poetry

Foreword

This is the third year that Leitrim County Council has put out a call for writing submissions from teenagers for inclusion in *Wild Words*, and by now the collection has become a fixture on the annual literary calendar. Though the standard of writing has remained as high as with *Volumes 1* and *2*, the number of entries has increased year on year; it's wonderful to see just how many young people from all across Ireland – and beyond – are interested in writing and committed enough to complete a piece of work and send it in to be assessed.

There was a real range of topics, themes and styles of writing submitted – from stylized Jazz Age pieces, police procedurals and gritty American-tinged realism, to dystopia, speculative fiction and narrative poetry – and it was very hard to narrow it down to the selection included here. Readers will find different pleasures in the pieces of writing included; some are little gems – short, but perfectly formed, others use a larger canvas and may one day develop into novels or longer stories. Some of the young writers have expressed themselves in very spare and simple words, while others are exploring how best to use language to express a mood or feeling. When trying to decide which submissions to include, I was looking out for well-handled ideas, gripping storylines, strong characters and an enjoyment of language and I think all the pieces in *Wild Words, Volume 3* display these.

Books published for this age group are often known as YA (Young Adult), and I think that the teenage authors included in *Wild Words, Volume 3* are all writing like young adults, rather than children. Their youth is apparent in the freshness of their writing and, in some pieces, the viewpoints and preoccupations of their protagonists, some of whom are finding their place in the world, dealing with choices about which road to take in life, or having problems with friends. Their move towards adulthood can be seen in the stories that deal with big themes like the environment, the causes of crime, death, loss, and having a family of their own. Many of these young writers are using their stories or poems to broaden their horizons and put themselves in others' shoes.

People often say 'write what you know', and while authenticity is important, I also like another maxim, 'write what you'd like to read'. I really get the feeling that that's what these writers have done, and in doing so they've created a book that many others will enjoy reading too.

So settle down with your copy of *Wild Words, Volume 3* and enjoy!

Helen Carr
August 2015

Helen Carr has worked in publishing for eighteen years and is Senior Editor with The O'Brien Press. She has worked with many Irish children's and YA authors, including Judi Curtin, Oisín McGann, Celine Kiernan, Alan Nolan, Erika McGann, Ruth Frances Long, Chris Judge and Sheila Agnew. Helen has also reviewed books for many publications, including *The Sunday Independent, Inis magazine* and *BookFest.*

PROSE

Barman's Blues

By Leesha Curtis, aged 15.

The year is 1921. John Harris felt this year was going to be his year. Neither his mother nor his father had wanted him to pursue his dream of becoming an actor. The idea to leave had come to him one night as he was tossing and turning in his four-poster bed. Now, here he was strolling down Fifth Avenue in New York City. He'd acquired a job at the Blue Flamingo bar, two blocks away from his motel. It wasn't much, but it would have to tide him over till he got his big break.

John glanced for the fifth time at the clock over the bar. He still had half an hour until closing time. If he was lucky no new customer would come in and he could leave a few minutes early and catch the last act in the theatre down the block. He counted down the minutes – ten, nine, eight, seven, six – but it wasn't meant to be. A tall, svelte brunette had just entered. She sashayed gracefully towards the bar, her bracelets jingling. Working at the bar for nearly five months now, John knew how to get people talking. Her name was Elizabeth Baker; he'd heard her name before. Her father owned several of New York's grandest hotels. She claimed to be eloping with one of her father's head clerks. 'He was just paralysed with happiness when I asked him,' she said. John chuckled, how typical of a bored heiress. 'Of course, my father will be furious, Tom's not that rich and I suppose we won't have much to live on for a spell, but I love him to bits,' she said carelessly. She fished around in her emerald-encrusted purse before letting a twenty-dollar bill float onto the bar's polished surface.

Mr. Alan Abbott, or Big Al to his friends, had worked as the Blue Flamingo's head barman for thirty years. When John, the new assistant barman, told him about Miss Elizabeth Baker he chuckled. Working in a bar for so long, he knew

5

everything about human nature. He knew why women laughed at older men's jokes, why the chef spat into the soups, and why young men working in bars could never be actors. John hadn't believed him when Al had said that Miss Baker's elopement wouldn't work out.

The year is now 1931. John nudges Big Al and nearly makes him drop his bottle of dry, eighteenth century, white wine. Ten years have passed since Miss Baker floated into the Blue Flamingo and yet here she is again, husband in tow. They are an odd couple; she is thin and graceful while he is short and pot-bellied. The two sit down at a table without a word. John gives Al a triumphant look but Al just shakes his head. He knows that when a man's bowler hat is dusty and unkempt, he is either of two things: a widower or someone who has lost the love of his wife. Al also knows that when a woman wears expensive shoes, whose only indication of age is on the soles, she is one of two things: a poor old maid or someone who has gone from riches to rags but doesn't want the world to know.

John walks down Fifth Avenue, he no longer strolls, saunters or bounds like he once did. His steady pace is disturbed when a street urchin, selling newspapers, drops a bunch of newspapers at his feet. John stares horrified at the front page, 'Elizabeth Baker, young heiress, murdered by husband.' John cannot move or speak or think. It was only two weeks since he had seen her sitting in front of him, at a small round table, with her husband.

Truly Excellent

By Johnjoe B. Gurry, aged 14.

From time to time I go to the flea market in Saint-Ouen, on the outskirts of Paris. It is a beautiful place, I find, because looking at all these marvels from other times, one has the impression of traversing the past while remaining in the present. But most of the past is not affordable to me. However, the last time I went, I discovered, in a narrow alleyway, a curious little shop. It was rather dilapidated and did not seem to have been painted for a long time, but it was somewhat charming. From what was left of the painting, one could make out 'Old Time Treasures - Antiques – Bric-A-Brac'. I crossed the threshold. There was everything in there: old grimoires (manuscripts), a Louis Philippe buffet, a Charles X dresser, old portraits, and boxes filled with trinkets. It was in rummaging through the latter that I unearthed three old alarm clocks and, deep down, a strange little box. It contained a beautiful little gold-plated Art Deco fountain pen in its original box. How wonderful! And it would change my life. I turned to the owner of the shop, a moustachioed sexagenarian sitting in a corner, smoking his pipe and asked:

'How much for this little lot?'

'What's in the little box?' he replied hoarsely.

'Thumbtacks,' I lied.

He reflected.

'I'll give you the lot for fifteen.'

'Twelve?'

'No, fifteen, they're old, these alarm clocks!'

'But they don't work! Come on, twelve is a very fair offer,' I insisted.

'Well ...'

And the deal was concluded. Delighted, I went home to properly examine my acquisitions. The alarm clocks were amusing. Once repaired, I could sell them for fifteen or twenty euros each. But the pen, ah, what a little treasure! I pulled out a sheet of paper from my drawers to see if it would still write. Although it was eighty years old, the ink was still black and fluid. I decided that I would use it for my French test the next day. When the time of the test arrived, I took out my pen and after reading the text of 'The Bewitched Jacket' by Buzzati, I began to answer the questions. Everything went perfectly, but when I returned to the first question, which I had passed over, something EXTRAORDINARY happened. I prepared to write my answer, 'One frequently finds in these texts a fantastic object ...' but I stopped to think some more. And now the pen completed my own answer, without the assistance of my hand. I was stunned, paralysed with amazement. I had to pinch myself several times to believe it. I overcame my emotions and verified the answer: it was perfect, flawless, even better than what I'd remembered from the lesson. But the magic of the pen didn't stop there. I reread the test and, for each question, the pen, under the influence of this mysterious charm, rose, as if to check with its non-existent eyes that the answer was one hundred percent correct. If it saw mistakes, it corrected each one without forgetting any. So many emotions were swirling around my mind as I looked on: joy, disbelief and pride among others.

The test took place on a Monday and the following Monday, the teacher gave out the results as I awaited with an incalculable degree of impatience. The only paper that got full marks was placed on my table. I was upset internally because I knew that I owed a good deal of my result to the pen. Throughout the first trimester, I used it for each test, with the same result. Curiously, no one spotted that the pen worked alone, probably an effect of the spell. And of course, my parents were extremely surprised by my school report because I obtained the best average in all subjects.

However, all good things come to an end, dear readers. While I was doing a Physics and Chemistry test, my pen stopped writing; there was no more ink. I finished the test with another pen. Rereading, I noticed that the pen no longer checked my answers. I then realised that the spell had gone. Definitively. But, dear readers, I was neither surprised nor sad. 'Why?' I hear you ask. For two reasons: firstly, the ink cartridges that it took are no longer available, and up to now, a pen cannot function without ink, nor the spell, of course. Secondly, we must simply accept that we cannot always excel in everything!

PS: The pen is superb, and it now adorns my office in memory of this adventure!

The Perfect Day

By Cian McGrath, aged 14.

It was when the perfect morning turned into the perfect day before ending with a majestic red sky that we held a picnic. Of course, the perfect morning had been easy to arrange. For breakfast, there were sausages that were just black enough to be jokingly labelled as a new 'charcoal' flavour, and white bread toast smeared with melted butter. That had been the easy part.

Then there was the visit to your mother's retirement home. It was one of the rare days when she could remember who we were, and one of the even rarer days when she left her bedside.

We walked outside and talked about how lovely the day was, as one of the more senile residents ran completely naked through the small back garden of the home, claiming that it was Ally land.

This situation became even more humorous and then alarming when he ran into one of the German residents, who just happened to sport a thick, bushy moustache, and only knew how to speak broken English.

The perfect day was harder to master, but still within the realms of possibility. There was a shopping trip, and a half-hour boat ride to an island that had no real distinction except for the fact that it had just been recently discovered. I remember you started sighing when you saw that a café was under construction there, stating that it was a manmade disgrace to nature.

A walk along the lakeside was also scheduled, and we fed ducks with a seemingly endless amount of brown bread, and I couldn't help feeling sorry for the fish underneath, who on rare occasions were gifted with meagre, soggy crumbs.

The arrangement for the perfect end to such a beautiful day had been significantly harder.

There was nothing to it, not really, but considering my ineptitude at baking/cooking/sandwich making, it was a miracle there was food.

In actual fact, the task was relatively easy. There were sandwiches to be made, which involved chicken breast and white bread with the crusts cut off, and cheese and tomato. The chicken was manageable, but the cheese proved harder than I had thought. I had considered grating, but dismissed the thought after remembering The Great Grater Disaster of '09, when more of my skin had been grated than actual cheese, causing the stuff to be a bizarre amalgamation of red and yellow.

But in the end, it was all there, in a small straw basket that rested on a newly bought blanket, on luscious green that overlooked mountains founded millions of years ago. I remember we both sat there, me picking off the stray pieces of tomato and you pretending to like the dreadfully bland chicken, as conversations containing various medical procedures loomed over us.

The conversation eventually turned to how long was left, and I hated every fibre of my being for asking it, and seeing your expression just broke my heart even more. But memories of your condition became so visually real that they hurt too much to hear.

I do not know what answer I expected, which was miraculous, as asking that one question plagued my every thought for days. I suppose it didn't really matter. The point was that we had each other, and we were together, and we were happy. The concept of more time was selfish and greedy, but there I was still a human part of me that clung onto it.

I remember you told me that exact thing, that time didn't matter, but in between starting a new conversation and ending this one, your eyes flashed with fear, the kind of fear that told me it was not a matter of months of weeks, and made my question whether the word 'days' was singular or plural.

But at that moment, I simply did not care. I knew that death was inevitable anyway, and that your passing would hurt just as much in the future as it would now. And in my heart of hearts, I knew the constant uncertainty of your condition would tear me apart, and I simply could not live with my life as though it were the last day.

And so, in the absence of a beautiful anti-climax, I looked in your eyes and smiled as the sun was setting and children were laughing and dogs were barking and the mountains stood tall above us, and I loved more then than I ever have.

Galaxies

By Jane McGlinchey, aged 15.

Silver stars scatter across the inky blackness above me as I gaze past the gnarled branches. The night breathes cool air on my neck as I lie nestled among the old roots. I have kept strong the last few hours since I heard the news, but now I break. A heavy sob rises from deep inside me to shake my whole body. We have spent summer nights under this tree for as long as the earth has orbited the sun, our thoughts and stories heard only by the stars light years away. Now the grass beside me feels empty and desolate. The night sky is cloudless yet memories fall as raindrops, cool and soothing on my burning mind. They are little pieces of you, making me feel less alone. I can almost hear your soft breathing in my ear and I let the wave of nostalgia wash over me. Times I had long forgotten about come flooding back.

When I got my tiny, white kitten and we were six years old, we both thought the world revolved around her. We missed two days of school because my mother couldn't get us to leave the back garden where we were playing with her. Hours were spent debating a name. Eventually we settled for Elska meaning 'love' in Icelandic as it was the native language of your grandmother. The grown Elska now pads up to me, curling herself protectively around my ankles. Again I close my eyes and remember a time, years later, when we thought you were moving across the country. In hushed whispers, we made as many plans as letters in the alphabet, a desperate attempt to make you stay. Turns out we were wrong all along, your parents were only planning a holiday, a surprise for your birthday.

Soon the sound of your soft breathing loudens, building to a crescendo of hyperventilation. Two years ago your mother passed away from cancer. Your tears spilt from an invisible crack that may have never healed. You didn't sleep for 48 hours and I sat with you the whole time as you cried until your soul ran dry. But you know what the worst thing is? Twenty-six months later the same thing happens. Only you are the one six feet under and I am left in bits, cold as shattered ice. And so I lie below our tree and look up at you, hidden within the galaxy of stars and whisper my last goodbye.

Reflection

By Ciara Brennan, aged 15.

There was always something strange about it.

I wanted an iPad. It's not as if I didn't drop enough hints. I knew I wanted an iPad around four months before my actual birthday. But that's my dad for you, if it's old he considers it valuable. I suppose that's probably to do with the fact that he is a history teacher. My mother, on the other hand, is a lot like myself. Not only do we look alike, we share the same views on dad's artefacts. Yet dad always manages to get his way, that's why our house is coming down with smelly old 'valuables'.

It was my fourteenth birthday. I was so sure dad had got me an iPad. I could hardly sleep the night before, I was so excited. Although that was the best night's sleep I got for a long time. I rushed down the stairs that morning, almost tripping over my own feet. I spilled into the sitting room where my mother and father were both waiting for me. That was the first time I laid eyes on it. It sent a sharp chill down my spine, my heart suddenly kick started into a faster pace. A mirror. I forced a smile and thanked my dad.

'I got it last month. I thought of you as soon as I saw it. It will be perfect for above the fireplace in your room!'

I remember mom giving me a hug and handing me my card. I had to drag my eyes off the mirror to check the card's contents. Fifty euro. I got the feeling the amount of money was designed to spite Dad, it's always a competition with those two.

Dad insisted in putting that mirror up by himself, he wouldn't accept any help. Mom offered and somehow it developed into an argument, it always does. After a few short hours, it was up. By that stage it was time for bed. I didn't want to go to bed. I didn't want to go into my own room.

My room had always been eerie, but this brought the eeriness to a new level. I felt like the mirror was watching me, waiting. The room was extra cold, and a powerful draft was pushing down the chimney, out into my room, chilling everything in its path. I braced myself. I went to fetch my toothbrush. I always brushed my teeth in the mirror, I told myself this would be no different. But I knew, I knew deep down.

I tiptoed up towards the mirror. From a distance, all looked pretty normal. There I was, in my same pyjamas. Holding my toothbrush in my mouth. I gained confidence, I moved closer. I looked away for a split second. I looked back into the mirror. My heart almost stopped. All I could do was scream. I didn't stop until my mother and father had their arms wrapped around me, reassuring me all was okay.

I'll never forget the face I saw staring back at me. In fact, it's impossible for me to forget. The face was swollen red. It looked hard, rough yellow in some areas. The face had bruises all over, black and blue. I froze, it felt like the face was mocking me. I explained exactly what I saw to my parents, neither of them believed me. They insisted it was a nightmare or I had imagined it. For the first time in months, they were agreeing.

I didn't sleep that night. Every time I closed my eyes, I saw it. I barely spoke to my parents that morning. The lump in my throat dried up any words on their way out. Honestly, I didn't want to speak. I nearly missed my bus that morning. Nearly. It took me several minutes longer than usual to get myself ready, as I was working without the use of a mirror.

I sat by myself that morning. Directly up the front, I didn't feel like speaking to anyone. My stomach was in knots, the yellow face played on my mind. Until my mind was silenced. Everything was silent. I didn't see it coming. A lorry. The silence was broken by helpless screams within seconds. That's all I remember from the accident. The silence. The screams. The silence.

It was six whole weeks before I was allowed to look into a mirror. My eyes had been covered in white bandages for the majority of the time. Six weeks did not feel long enough. I knew. I came face to face with a mirror, I didn't have to look. Burns. A nurse tweeted in my ear that time heals and I came out okay considering.

The yellow face. This time it wasn't going anywhere.

The Worst Holiday Ever

By Jane McGlinchey, aged 15.

The air is still. Still and cool. I don't like it one bit. I continue through the forest along the path of rubbery shrubs I used to know so well. The tall, straight trees either side of me no longer feel protecting, instead they look down on me.

A smell of rot fills my nose as I try to figure out why the silence bothers me so much. Seconds later, it hits me like a stone. The animals. The ants and monkeys and spiders, every colour of the rainbow. They are gone. I take a deep breath, in through the nose, out through the mouth. 'Maybe what they said was true.' I speak the words out loud, an attempt to believe what I am saying. Or maybe just to break the eerie quiet.

I cast my mind back to when the reports were first published. Everyone thought the President was cracked, first off for believing what the biologists told him, then for declaring a worldwide holiday. In his words, 'If this really is the end of time, we may as well enjoy every second we have left'. But what was he expecting? A national bungee-jumping binge? Everyone has their bucket-list, be it charity work or cliff diving, but in the end, everyone has eyes bigger than their belly.

I notice how the snowdrops are beginning to wilt, yet it's only early spring. For the first time, I wonder where the animals have gone. They aren't dead, I would smell it if they were dead. I let this perplex me for several minutes, not wanting to target the thought of what lies ahead. Or what doesn't, if all this is true.

Eventually I give in and the anger, confusion and helplessness wash over me in tsunami tides. It's a strange thing being told the earth is dying. It had seemed indestructible. For eons it watched every human being attempt to make it to the top of this concrete jungle, only to walk straight into inevitable death. The earth sustained quadrillions of living creatures, from the first fifty-foot dinosaur to the very last bacterium and, even though we as humans have spent millennia destroying our planet, killing, killing, killing, we never thought it would die. The earth was assumed to be as immortal as the Gods we've created. But the studies have taken everything we see as truth and buried it alongside our loved ones in the ground.

The scientists say the sun no longer gives off enough energy to keep us alive. I look skywards at the small orange sphere. It almost feels darker than five minutes ago, but it couldn't be happening this fast, could it? I brush off the thought.

The energy we currently have is quickly being wasted as heat. The government could find a way to conserve the energy if it weren't for the fact that they are all off work to enjoy whatever time is left. It must be the worst holiday ever, carrying the knowledge that you are going to die soon. Soon. Not when. That part is most horrible, not knowing when.

I am nearing the edge of the forest and through the trunks I see the grey ocean. The tide-less water is a mirror of still, the moon too tired to drag it around the globe. I reach the soft sand and hunker down, pulling my wool coat tighter around my shoulders. My dark hair falls limply down my back, a waterfall of ink.

I don't know what to expect now. Floods, earthquakes? The sky is as cloudless as the deserts that have taken most of our land and nothing on this earth has moved in days.

I sit on the shores for what could be hours or minutes. A strange numbing sensation begins to take hold of my body. The air is arctic cold, yet I feel strangely warm. The sight is beginning to fade from my eyes, the colours running into each other, until everything is pale grey. I can no longer feel the sand beneath me, in fact I feel nothing at all. I should be panicking but tranquillity covers me like a blanket.

And then it dawns on me. This is the end. No torrents of water pouring from the heavens, no large cracks in the ground swallowing anyone who dares go near, not even a last visit from the Creator.

But its ok, it feels right. I realise that this is the perfect way to end. Nature never did make a big deal of itself. Always there, silently observing, beautiful just in what it was. The last of the light fades, until

They're Coming

By Scott Green, aged 17.

I fumble with the switch on the camera waiting for the flashing light which indicates it has started recording. I look at the locked door of the lab. They're coming. They're coming for me. I switch my attention to the lens of the camera. 'I will not try to justify what we've done here. Our experiment was unethical at the best of times. Of course that is not to say the populace disagreed. Oh no, quite the opposite. They practically cheered when we said we had a way to take care of the excess criminals who were bursting out of our prisons. They brushed it under the carpet when we accidentally went too far with one of our patients. It was only when we required ordinary members of society that they turned on us. Suddenly what we were doing was "wrong" and we were portrayed as monsters.' A particularly loud bang draws my attention to the door again. I furrow my brow. 'Hmm, it appears I may not have much time left. I fear I've been sidetracked by my criticism of the outside world. I apologize for my team's actions of course. We should not have played God. We should not have tampered with the delicate system that is the human body, but we needed to know how fine the line between man and beast was.'

I remove my glasses and wipe them on my lab-coat, I hold them up to the light before resuming. 'As we discovered,' I sigh, 'the line is extremely thin. We knew the dangers of our experiments. Electroshock therapy has always been criticized due to the psychological damage it can inflict, but we pushed these worries aside. We needed to know what it would take to push someone over the line; we needed to find the breaking point. 'And we found it,' I smiled wryly, 'by God we found it. All it took was a direct current of thirty-one volts to send someone into an animalistic rage. Our testing concluded it was due to an abnormally large production of adrenaline.

Unsatisfied with this our patrons demanded we repeat the experiment over and over again on a wide variety of patients.'

I wipe my glasses again and I can feel the beads of sweat that are starting to trickle down my forehead. 'The results were unprecedented, the foreign adrenaline attached to cells in a way we'd never even dreamt of.' The banging on the door grows louder and more frantic. I can see it start to bend under the sustained pressure. 'Except for in nightmares. The patients became uncontrollable and even broke some of the restraints we placed on them. They' I hold back tears, 'they ripped one of my assistants apart. And bit off another's fingers. The horrors didn't end there. After we had [ahem] disposed of the remains of my first assistant, the other started to undergo changes. He complained of sight problems, headaches and became extremely short-tempered. It climaxed when he attempted to strangle one of the janitors. The mutation seemingly removes the hosts' ability to recognize friend from foe and so leads to them attacking anyone in sight. What's worse is any victim who isn't horribly dismembered is converted and the cycle repeats. It appears that any transferral of bodily fluids from a host to a victim is enough to kick-start the mutation in said victim. The mutated cells act similarly to virus cells. First they attach themselves to the nearest cell and convert it to a virus cell and the cycle repeats until the virus cells are in the majority at which point the disease takes control of the victim. The process is extraordinarily quick compared to that of known diseases taking a mere twenty-seven minutes to take hold. At present there is no cure aside from the destruction of the victim's vital organs.'

The door finally appears as though it is about to crumple under the sustained pounding it has been receiving and I begin to shake. They're almost here. 'I only hope that the outside world can stop these monsters we've created.' The door breaks and a horde of infected humans barrel into the room. 'May God forgive us.'

They're here.

The Prism Power

By Katie Soden, aged 16.

Max Crawford was born with a strange secret. His friends didn't know it existed, or his parents, or even he himself. Today however, was the day the secret lying dormant within him would come to light and the world he knew would be shattered by its arrival.

Max had gotten into a fight at school today. The fifteen-year-old was currently slumped on a park bench scrolling through his phone after walking out of the school. He probably looked like a delinquent with a bruise on his right cheek and red raw knuckles that made him look like he had been in a fist fight (which he had). He had watchful hazel eyes that peered out under a fringe of black hair that stuck up like a mad bird's nest. Max Crawford found it difficult to blend in. This probably stemmed from his scruffy appearance and his 'I-couldn't-care-less personality', but mostly from the very visible birthmark he had. He was born with a dark red birthmark that had crawled its way down from the left side of his face onto his neck, then his shoulder, over his arm and ended at the very tips of his fingers. It was shaped in a pattern of detached red splotches and sat flat against his skin.

As you can imagine, and probably remember, school is a horrible place and being born with such a stand-out feature was practically equal to having a giant 'kick me' sign strapped to your back 24/7. Max had always covered up his left hand with a fingerless glove seeing as how he had a strange mark on his palm. It was shaped like a triangle and when some twat had ripped off the glove he covered it with to get a look, he wasn't too happy about it. Max didn't take kindly towards people prodding him and staring so he took this opportunity to punch the boy as hard as possible. He got into a little scuffle which resulted in him eventually escaping out the window to avoid the principal's wrath and legging it out of the school.

He heard a gasp come from beside him and looked up from his phone. A girl with blonde hair scraped into a bun sat beside him, her hands clasped over her mouth and her blue eyes blown wide staring at him. She was wearing a green jacket, a white vest, and black shorts and was... barefoot.

She was staring at him, her mouth hanging open.

Max felt his anger flare. Great, another idiot who wanted to gawk at the town freak. She wasn't even trying to hide it!

'It's a birthmark, you know.' He growled. 'It's not contagious so you don't have to worry about it infecting you.'

'Oh.' She said quietly. 'So, you can't regenerate?'

Max's head snapped up. 'What?' He asked, bewildered.

'If it's something you were born with you probably can't fix it.' She said, sitting back in the bench. 'Maybe you don't need to fix it. It's a bit odd but I'm friends with lots of odd people.' She responded staring off into the sky.

Max stared at this girl with an expression of disbelief. Was she mocking him? She was acting kind of odd and—

Oh.

The penny dropped. She... probably wasn't all there in the head exactly. Sitting on a park bench barefoot and staring at strangers wasn't exactly normal behaviour.

Well, now I feel like a prick. He thought.

'Um, excuse me, what's your name?' He asked.

'Arietta.' She said quietly.

'Right, Arietta, are you by any chance lost or need help getting back home?'

'Oh no, I'm waiting here for some friends!' She chirped, taking a walkie talkie from her back pocket.

'So you'll be ok? They're people you know?' He asked, wondering why she used a walkie talkie instead of a phone.

Max was so engrossed in his conversation he didn't notice the dingy red car that rounded the block and pulled up in front of the two.

'Yes. Thanks for your concern.' She replied.

'Max!' A voice called out.

He looked to see who it was calling his name and when he set his eyes on the dingy red vehicle before him his heart stopped. He wouldn't have been so shocked had it not been for the fact that the voice calling his name belonged to someone very important to him. Someone who had died two years ago.

For the first time in two years Max laid his eyes on his half-brother Zeke sitting in the front seat of the red car.

'Max,' Zeke called out urgently, 'get in. We gotta talk.'

'Bye!' Arietta said as the boy drifted in a dreamlike state towards the car.

He looked in the front passenger window to check it was really him. Max took in his brothers tanned skin, brown eyes and blonde hair. He must be twenty by now.

'Oh my god, Zeke, it's you. It's really you!' He gasped, flinging open the passenger door and wrapping his arms around him. Zeke hugged him back for a moment and pried the boy off of him, gripping his shoulders. He had a sternness in his eyes Max rarely saw.

'Max, I have a lot to explain but first I have to show you something. Close the door, I'll talk while I drive'.

Max shut the door, giddy with excitement as a million questions swirled around his mind. The car sped down the street and Max turned to look at his brother.

'Zeke, where have you been for the past two years? Everyone thought you were dead! Why didn't you come back? How are you still alive?'

'This is gonna take a while to explain. You can have some coffee while I explain.' He said, pointing at the cup holder.

'This is crazy! Oh my god I- I have to call mom and dad!' He cried, pulling out his mobile.

'No.' Zeke's voice cut in firmly as he plucked the phone out of Max's hands.

'No? What do you mean no?'

Zeke didn't respond.

Max felt panic rise in his chest. Why was his brother being so secretive? The Zeke he remembered was always straight with Max. What was he hiding?

He caught a glimpse of a sign as they drove on saying 'You are now leaving Linfort town'. They were driving towards the woods.

'Zeke, are you in some kind of trouble?' Max asked, his voice tainted by panic.

His half-brothers face twitched, but he continued to stare straight ahead, ignoring Max.

'Zeke tell me. Did you get tied up in something bad? Are there people after you? Did you go into hiding? Is that why you couldn't come home?' He asked frantically.

No reply.

'ZEKE WILL YOU JUST TELL ME WHAT THE HELL YOU DID!?!' He screamed.

'You should drink some coffee.' He said calmly as if he couldn't hear his brother practically roaring at him.

Max was sure something was horribly wrong. His relief and excitement had been replaced by a sickening anxiety twisting and writhing in his gut. He looked at his brother, trying to pick out what it was that seemed so strange to him. He had the same piercings in his ear, the same tanned skin and the same eyes. He... he hadn't changed much for someone that had been gone for two years. He didn't know how but he knew something was off. His instincts were screaming at him to do something. What was his brother hiding?

If this even is his brother.

Every second he wasted sitting here thinking was a second the car sped on further away from town and closer to the woods. His brother seemed very eager to get Max to drink this coffee. He kept insisting so Max decided to play along. He had to figure out if this really was Zeke or not. If this was going to work he had to be smart about it.

He looked at the small opening in the coffee cup and lifted it to his mouth. He turned it slightly in his hand and sucked on the rim, making it look like he was sipping it. He felt the driver's eyes looking at him and his stomach churned but didn't dare check.

'Hey, Zeke,' He started, fingers firmly clutching the cups lid.

'Yeah?'

'Have you called your girlfriend Monica recently?' He asked, glancing out the window.

'No. I couldn't talk to her. I was too busy, but I will call her later if you want me to.'

That was it. He turned to the driver and looked him in the eye.

'Monica's been dead for the past five years.'

The driver's eyes widened with alarm and his grip clenched the steering wheel.

Max reacted first. He pried the lid off the coffee cup and flung the steaming coffee into the driver's eyes. He screamed in pain and Max unbuckled his seat belt turning and opening the car door. The car swerved violently and a hand sharply tugged Max by the back of his shirt collar away from the door hanging wide open. He pinned Max against his side, his arm clenched around his neck in a vice like grip. Max bucked and kicked, screaming and clawing helplessly at the kidnapper's arm. He looked around to see if there was anyone who could hear him screaming and that's when he saw it.

Arietta was standing in the middle of the road.

The doppelganger's face cracked into a horrid demented smile and he pressed down on the accelerator.

'Arietta! RUN!' Max screamed, slamming the horn with his fist. Arietta looked up and for a second and Max caught a glimpse of her expression: stern and determined. She didn't jump out of the way.

She jumped *towards* them.

As she leaped into the air, something strange happened. In a flicker, the skin on her legs and arms turned from fair to a steely grey. Her left arm shaped into a conical silver spike and reared back.

She landed on the front of the car, her feet cutting into the bonnet and cementing her in place. Her blade arm sprung forward and shattered the windscreen, slicing into the kidnapper's shoulder. He cried out but no blood leaked from the wound. Max screamed in terror as glass exploded everywhere, trying to lurch away in spite of the seemingly unbreakable grip the driver had on him. Arietta aimed another stab at the driver, her electric blue eyes livid.

The car swerved suddenly and her arm snapped past the drivers face, shattering the window beside him. Her other arm dug into the roof of the car, the steel fingers piercing through the metal. His arm tightened around Max's neck, cutting off his screams and squeezing him so tight he thought his neck was going to snap. Max saw a flash of silver fly over his head cutting into the seat as it flew past. The pressure around his neck immediately dropped and he heard a horrible keening metallic scream come from behind him. Whatever this thing was it sure as hell wasn't human.

Max wasted no time pushing the detached arm off of himself and scrambling to the car door. For a moment as he held the door open he considered the madness of the situation. Jumping out of a moving car swerving madly wasn't exactly a good idea. He looked back and saw the doppelganger trying to fight off Arietta, screeching and snapping at her viciously. Half of its face had been torn off and as it whirled around to face him he saw the silver endoskeleton beneath the flesh. It screamed and lunged at him, its jaw open and fingers poised like claws.

Max jumped.

He landed painfully, scraping his hands on the gravel as he tumbled onto the road. He groaned in pain and climbed to his feet, picking the grit out of his bloody palms. The car was out of control and heading towards a tree. Arietta abandoned the fight and dashed over the top of the car. She landed on the road as the car crashed, the bonnet buckling as it collided with the tree. She sprinted towards Max, stopping a few feet away from him. The car door opened and the kidnapper staggered out. It seemed to be clutching some sort of large gun it must have hidden in the back seat.

'Stay back, Max! I'll handle this.' Arietta insisted, her arms shaped into spikes. The doppelganger stood about twelve paces from them. Max felt his stomach churning. Someone had tried to kidnap him. They had used his dead brother against him and tricked him into believing he was back. Now a nightmarish parody of his brother stood before him, half of his face ripped off and one of his arms missing. It felt almost like he was being mocked, teased with the idea of his brother surviving the incident long ago only to have it revealed to be a cruel ploy to kidnap him. He didn't want to see this. It was sick. He didn't want to remember Zeke like this.

He would never own up to it, but Max idolized his brother.

He remembered Zeke spending the whole day playing with him on Max's tenth birthday because no one came to the party.

He remembered Zeke beating up boys twice the size of himself for calling his little brother a freak.

He remembered Zeke never treating him differently for how he looked and always taking time to listen to him.

He remembered Zeke protecting him, watching out for him, trying to make him feel like he was worth something and challenging anyone who dared hurt his little brother.

Then some imposter comes along, not only trying to kidnap him but using the image of his dead brother to do it?

That was it.

'Who… the hell…are you?' He snarled, his fists clenched so hard his knuckled turned white.

The triangle on Max's hand began to pulse beneath the black fingerless glove, a red glow emitting from the palm. The glow spread up his arm illuminating only the splotched birthmark pattern. He pulled off the glove out of instinct, the glow spreading higher and higher, growing stronger until it reached his face. Arietta was staring at Max, transfixed by the sight she was seeing. He held out his arm and the power coiled inside his palm sprung into life.

A circle of white light formed in front of his palm, seven triangles spread evenly throughout the ring. The triangles were red, orange, yellow, green, blue, indigo and violet.

This wasn't a normal situation, but Max was not thinking normally either. All he was thinking about was destroying the creature that had used the image of his dead sibling against him. He didn't know how he did what he did next, but all he recalls is that it flowed naturally, as if he had done it before. An old knowledge long forgotten was returning to him.

He touched three of the different colours, the mark on his palm taking three of these layers stacking them horizontally. Red, yellow and orange.

His arm pulsed yellow and Max ran towards the imposter, his speed much faster than that of an ordinary human. Yellow light trailed his hands and feet like shadows as he moved. His left eye now glowed yellow. The doppelganger shot the strange gun several times at him. The blasts weren't bullets but some sort of neon red laser beams. Max evaded every blast dashing and swerving with ease. He practically flew towards him dodging a punch and pressing his glowing hand against the robot's stomach. His fury lent him strength and a beam of red light shot out sending the robot flying off of the ground and across the road. His arm and eye was now pulsing red, crimson flowing from his hands and feet like smoky fins. His birthmark, eye and light trails seemed to switch colour depending on the most recent power he used.

'You're using it...' Arietta spoke in awe, her voice timid and quaking with excitement. 'The prism power.'

Max gazed at the triangle glowing on his hand. 'The prism power?' He repeated.

'Look out!' She yelled.

The robot was charging towards him. Max pulsed orange, dodging the robot and shooting out an orange cord out of his hand. It coiled around the robot's legs and he fell. The kidnapper turned over to try and untangle himself but Max didn't give him a chance. He shot out an orange spike that sliced into its hand, pinning the palm to the ground.

His face contorted with fury, Max pulsed red and started firing blast after blast at the helpless robot. It let out shrill pained screams writhing in agony as it was attacked

31

relentlessly. Arietta's excitement faded to fear as she watched. Max's entire body was quaking and a demented glint shone in his eyes.

'Max, it's dead. You have to deactivate your powers.' She said with more confidence than she felt.

Max raised his head and looked at her, fear in his eyes. 'I can't.' He gasped, his arm pulsing violet.

The seven colours began swirling around in a spiral around his feet as Max staggered away from the robot.

'I killed him…' He whimpered, shivering. 'I KILLED MY BROTHER!'

The swirling colour suddenly exploded around him. The robot's inanimate corpse was flung far away while Arietta was barely hanging on to where she stood. She shielded her eyes with her arms, turning her legs to steel to weigh herself down.

A vicious spiral of light swirled around Max, his arm, eye and trails glowing violet. The spiral was all of the seven colours spiking and falling into the ground like a ferocious ocean. He was in the eye of a tornado of light, his skin cracking. He looked at the seams and he saw they weren't red but black.

'MAX, YOU'RE GOING TO DIE! YOU HAVE TO DEACTIVATE IT! PLEASE!' She screamed.

'I can't.' He cried, turning to her. His eyes were pitch black. He wasn't in control anymore.

'HOW DO I STOP IT!?'

'I-I don't know!' She responded.

'WHAT THE HELL DO YOU MEAN YOU DON'T KNOW?' He screamed furiously. His skin cracked even more, the spiral becoming more vicious.

'How can you not know?' He yelled, his eyes watering. 'I have no idea what's going on! I don't know what any of this means! Where is my real brother? Is he dead? Who was that guy and what was he going to do to me? Who are you? *What* are you? Can I even trust you?'

Max was beginning to feel very cold, the cracks travelling and growing over his body as his panic rose.

'You can trust me! I have friends that can help you! I know where your real brother is.'

'NO YOU CAN'T! YOU'RE A LIAR! I KILLED MY BROTHER RIGHT HERE!' He screamed. The marks spread further over his body.

Max was rapidly losing his body and mind while Arietta was beyond panicking. The power was overwhelming him. She wasn't trained to handle this. It was supposed to be a simple retrieval mission. He was on his knees with his head in his hands and tears streaming down his cheeks from onyx eyes. His chest felt hollow

She was scared, but he was losing himself. Arietta stopped shaking. She was meant to bring him back safe, no matter what. She began to walk towards the coloured tornado, shouting over the noise the raging spiral made.

'MAX! LISTEN TO ME! THIS IS YOUR POWER. YOU CONTROL IT, IT DOESN'T CONTROL YOU.' He looked up, his face covered with a spider web of cracks. 'ALL OF THIS IS NEW TO YOU AND IT'S OVERWHELMING. I KNOW HOW YOU FEEL BUT YOU'RE STRONGER THAN THIS!' He looked up at her and she saw she was getting through to him. 'YOU'RE GOING TO DO SO MANY AMAZING THINGS! YOU'RE GOING TO HELP SO MANY PEOPLE! I KNOW YOU CAN BEAT THIS! I BELIEVE IN YOU MAX!'

Max's skin was deathly pale, his entire body covered with black seams. He closed his onyx eyes and focused. This energy was his. This life was his. This power was his.

He was going to take back control.

Max held out both of his hands with his palms facing upwards. The tornado did not waver but pieces of light from the base began to split from the spiral around him. Flickers of red, orange, yellow, green, blue, indigo and violet began to flow into his palms. First it was random fly away flickers but it grew into a steady stream. His eyes opened wide flickering between hazel and black as his birthmark shone white. The energy was overwhelming, the sheer force of it indescribable as it shot into his palms and returned within him. He felt himself straining under the weight. The power was bringing him to his knees. Every part of him wanted to collapse, but he wouldn't give in. Shaking, straining and exhausted, he forced himself up and stood tall, the energy pouring into his palms. His hands shook as the tornado lessened. It faded and faded but he stayed standing, refusing to give up. After what seemed like a lifetime, the last remaining pieces of light were sucked into his palm.

Arietta stood slack-jawed in awe. He slowly lowered his hands to his sides. His skin was back to normal and there were no cracks in it or hints of darkness in his eyes. His birthmark glowed white and then faded back to its normal dark red colour. Exhausted both physically and emotionally, he looked towards Arietta and gave her a genuine smile.

'Thank you.'

She cracked a grin as well. They stood there for a moment in silence. Max took a step towards Arietta when he suddenly stumbled and fell. Arietta managed to catch him before he hit the ground. She laid him down and checked his pulse and breathing. He was stable. Arietta let out a sigh. She pulled a walkie talkie out of her pocket and began to speak.

'This is blade dancer coming in, repeat, blade dancer coming in. The target has been secured. Target is unconscious but stable. No human casualties, one hostile robotic creation annihilated. Over.'

'Roger that. Sending transport right now. Will arrive in roughly twenty minutes to your area. Over.'

On the other end of the line, Zeke Crawford clutched the walkie talkie to his chest. He smiled as he fought to supress a swirl of emotions welling up inside of him.

I knew you could do it, little brother. I always knew you could. He thought.

Zeke laid the walkie talkie on the table, collapsing into a chair and letting out a breath he didn't know he was holding. He pulled a frayed photo out of his pocket. It was an image of his little brother Max smiling at the camera.

'You know things are going to get a lot harder for him.' A voice spoke out from behind him.

Zeke turned to look at his squad leader, Sting. He was tall and strong built with cropped brown hair and sharp eyes. The man was in his mid-twenties, perched on stool in the corner sharpening a dagger with a sharpening stone. He kept talking without looking up.

'What he faced there is nothing compared to what he'll be fighting in the future. Your baby brother might have his magic powers to protect him but things are only going get harder from this point on.' He sat forward and set his hard eyes on Zeke.

'You really think he's going to be able to lead this rebellion? Do you really think he's going to be able to stop the organization that's after us? That's after him? If they get their hands on him they'll destroy him.'

'I know my brother, Sting. He'll back us up.' Zeke replied confidently.

'He can't just fight in this war. He has to want to be here. He has to view us as equals. Not just as mutants but as people. You know what we're going up against and if he's not with us our whole battle will be for nothing. We're not all like that Blade Dancer girl. Not all of us can look or act entirely human. Is he going to think of us as freaks?'

'My brother was treated like a freak his whole life for his birthmark.' Zeke said sharply. 'Kids used to throw rocks at him when he walked home. He grew up with people asking him if his mark was contagious. He avoids mirrors and I've seen him wince at his own reflection. He's not going to care what we look like. I haven't seen Max in two years. He might have changed a bit but if there is one thing I know about Max it's that he cares about who a person is, not what they are. Mutant or human, it wouldn't make a difference to him.'

'Even still, this is a lot of pressure for a kid. Be honest with me Zeke, is he going to be able to fight in this war?'

'He's not just going fight in this war.' Zeke said, looking up from the photo.

'He's going to win it.'

Stations of the Cross

By Alana Mahon O'Neill, aged 17.

The most dangerous stations are the emptiest.

'I was with your grandfather for forty-two years before he had that stroke in the middle of Dunne's Stores. I was always telling him to put more linseed into his cereal, but ah, sure it's too late now.'

I stretched my mouth into a strained smile that probably looked like a tortured grin. I only felt relieved that the church was now mostly empty and only a few bystanders turned to address the odd shrill voice. I pretended not to notice and my grandmother never considered any possibility that she spoke louder than the priest when she would ask me to pass the leaflet. One moment the priest was saying, 'May the Lord be with you' and next the congregation was muffled by, 'THIS IS YESTERDAY'S LEAFLET. THEY PRINTED THE WRONG READINGS. IT'S ALL LIES. ALL LIES.'

Thank God, most people ignored her. Nevertheless I burned with embarrassment as girls from school sniggered at the opposite end of the cathedral. I often prayed that I would accustom to my grandmother's exuberant, overly-extroverted, displays of annoyance over little, trivial matters. Unfortunately, I was more self-conscious than my grandmother.

'Do you see them, up there?' she pointed upwards to the pictures on the wall showing Jesus carrying his cross, 'I remember when they put these up and your man who made them.'

'Yes, Granny.'

'He's dead now.'

'I guessed.'

The church was completely empty now with the priest outside talking to parishioners who took great interest in GAA matches and dead people. My grandmother, meanwhile, still sat, scrutinizing the images above us. She glared with such solemnity like a detective trying to find a criminal's fingerprints that I immediately turned my attention towards the oil paintings, yet could not find anything of significance.

'What is it?' I asked.

'I don't suppose you know each station of the cross, do you?'

'He gets the cross, goes there, dies then comes alive again?' I suggested.

'There are fourteen.'

THERE ARE FOURTEEN?

'No, I don't think I can.' I admitted.

'Don't worry.' She said, 'I can't either.'

I think I nearly died.

'Yes.' She said, 'I remember being in mass, with Fr. O'Byrne still saying it, with your mother when she was your age. Sure, she had to be dragged along by tooth and nail. You're much better for going to mass.'

Now, of course, was not a time to mention that I attended mass to be civil and that I had little to no interest in organised religion and merely attended to accompany her and to keep her happy. The ramp upwards towards the church was too steep for my grandmother to do on her own, especially on wet days. One winter's day when the ground was particularly icy, she made a race at the ramp, knocking small children out of the way. With great power she reached the top of the ramp, victorious, then immediately began to slide back down again. 'FOR GOD'S SAKE!' she yelled while I pushed her up, bright red and sweating in humiliation.

'My mother went to mass?' I questioned innocently, though I knew from family stories that my mother was an adamant atheist with a passion.

My grandmother nodded, pursing her thin lilac lips in a melancholic manner, 'Ah sure, she lost her way, eventually. Me and Brendan were on to her for ages and ages to come down to go, just the once, but she wasn't having it. I didn't hear from her for a while then. Not until the cancer and your man leaving.'

'Do you ever suppose my dad's still around somewhere?'

'That eejit, love? You're better off not knowing him. God rest his soul.'

'He's not dead, Granny.'

'Well, I hope he is. HO, HO, shouldn't be saying that here. Never mind. You know fellas like that; they last twice the age they're supposed to.'

'I suppose.' I said, though I didn't really know how to respond to the comment.

We sat in silence. It grew chilly and I shivered but my grandmother was unmoved, particularly as she wore a blue shawl and blanket across her legs. I longed for the moment in which her hands would reach either side of her as she made a motion to leave. Yet, her hands lay resolutely clasped in her lap.

'Do you remember anything of your mother?' she asked me. I shook my head. She sighed, 'Well, how young you were…that's just the way it is.'

'Do you miss her?'

'Every day.' She said.

'I miss her too.'

'It's a crime that a child should not know their parents, well that cannot be helped.'

She stared up at the images for a long time.

'Do you like them?' I asked.

'No.' she whispered, bitterly, 'I hate them.'

My grandmother, no matter what, was unwavering in her beliefs. She prayed for souls in purgatory, for souls that were once and eventually would be in this limbo. She prayed for the living and the dead, and considered these better than praying for herself. I was surprised to find her hating something so suddenly and so ferociously.

'Why?' I asked, and then shook my head. No, she was too stressed out and too tired, 'Look, forget what I said-'

'They remind me of my daughter, of your mother.' She sighed and pulled her blanket further up her lap and twisted on the corners of it with her fingers.

'How?' I asked.

My mother was merely an average, young woman. I looked at the grotesque, baroque influenced panoramic scenes of Jesus's final day alive. I grew worried, wondering how my grandmother had drawn relativity to my mother's life from such a horrible image.

I did not want to ask, but the question I had unfolded into the air like a heavy stench for her to answer and I would rather be at home, at that moment rather than talk about something which was so uncomfortable.

'You know your mother was in Dublin.' My grandmother elaborated, 'I did not even know she had you, or had cancer, until I got the phone call. Her husband left her with you, as a young child. She had no money and no intention to connect back home. She wasn't able to afford chemotherapy and didn't even attend any support groups. The doctors gave her sleeping pills and she overdosed from misreading. Well, I never told you this, but I think you are old enough now: I hope she misread.'

I knew the story. I suspected it myself and it felt like nothing, but I knew it was a lot to her.

'Murderers and rapists can get into heaven but those who murder themselves, cannot. That worries me every day. That no matter what, I cannot pray for my lost child. I look at this picture every day and I am constantly reminded. Christ died for our sins, by his own hand; he descended into hell, but on the third day rose again. I only hope it could be true.'

I wondered how I could comfort a deeply devout woman that religion may not be as black and white as it is made out to be and that there cannot be a clear set of scripture as those try to interpret. It was an action of holding back a sea with my bare hands. I could not change something that was set in stone. So, like a coward, I remained obtuse. I remained silent.

Maybe she wanted it that way.

'So, there are fourteen stations.' I said.

'Yes,' my grandmother nodded.' I noticed her wipe her eyes with her shaking hand, but pretended I did not see anything. 'It does not matter that you do not know every single one. Just notice how at every one, Jesus had his followers. Those who loved him. Even when condemned to death he had those who helped carry his cross and pick him up when he fell. His station was full. While your mother's was empty. She did not allow anybody to settle in it and people came into her life then left. And maybe that's what the difference is.'

We sat in stone cold silence until Fr. O'Byrne came strolling in.

'Lovely day, isn't it?'

'Ah, sure, it's a fine day.' My grandmother laughed as if the previous conversation never took place, 'Going to go home and make myself a cup of tea, once this lad gets going!'

I WAS WAITING FOR HER THIS WHOLE TIME!

'Well, just to be sure that you close the latch after yourself!' the priest said.

'Oh, yeah, sure.' She chirped, 'You don't want anybody coming in here and praying!'

They both laughed hysterically while I pondered whether or not a priest's reaction would be the same if I said something along the same lines or whether I'd be kicked out on my backside. Meanwhile, my grandmother suddenly bowled down the ramp at a breakneck speed and nearly fell out of her chair as she crashed into neatly trimmed hedge.

April

By Emma Costello, aged 16.

18th May, 2008; a cloudless morning. The sun shone brightly onto the trees, making them glitter like gold. Birds swooped across the sky, chirping happily. Little kids screamed with delight as they rode their bikes down the street, ringing their bells cheerily.

It was a Sunday; my only day off from work. I had a whole day to spend with my daughter, April. I smiled at the thought. It was just the two of us; April's dad had been killed in a plane crash in 2001. She was only a few months old at the time.

I slid out of bed, and went into April's room. As you would expect from a seven-year-old girl, it was littered with princess dolls and pink girly things. I crept towards her bed, bent down, and softly tickled her cheek. She stirred underneath the covers and then opened her eyes.

'Morning, mommy,' she whispered sleepily.

'Morning, princess,' I replied, stroking her long, blonde hair. 'Wanna get some breakfast?'

She nodded and then slid out of bed. We went into the kitchen, yawning as we walked. While April sat at the table, I poured us some juice; orange for me, apple for April. I turned to her. 'What cereal would Miss April like this morning, then?'

'Um... FROSTIES!' she shouted, giggling. Frosties were her favourite.

'All right then!' I said, giggling myself. I peered into the cereal cupboard, but there wasn't a Frosties box in sight.

'Sorry, honey,' I said, 'but we don't have any Frosties.'

April pulled a sad face and then smiled. 'Can we *please* go to the shop and get some, Mommy?'

I sighed, but agreed.

'Get changed first, though. We don't want people seeing us in our pyjamas!'

April laughed.

We drove into the town of Saltlake, just outside Chicago city. Saltlake is a good community. People have always been good to me, especially when April's dad died.

I parked right outside the shop door. The car park was empty; most people were probably at church.

I kissed April's forehead. 'I'll just be two minutes, okay?' April nodded.

I ran into the shop, and grabbed the first box of Frosties I saw. Handing two dollars to the shopkeeper and yelling 'Keep the change!' I raced back out the door. I climbed back into the car, slamming the door shut. 'Here's your Frosties, honey!' I said, turning to April.

But April wasn't there.

I dropped the box of cereal and screamed. Shaking, I ran out of the car, and into the shop.

'Call 911, please!' I screamed to the shopkeeper, my eyes blurred with tears. 'My daughter's gone, please help me!'

The last thing I remember is collapsing on the floor, choking back tears, and whispering her name over and over again.

* * *

'Miss Wood? *Miss Wood?*' I open my eyes to see a woman, around my age, kneeling beside me. Her brown hair was pulled back into a ponytail, and her hand was on my right shoulder.

I frantically sat up on the sofa I was lying on, looking around the room.

'M-my daughter, April... she's gone, you have to find her...'

'I know,' said the woman, 'we're looking for her. My name is Detective Johnson, I'm with the FBI. Do you know what happened to April?'

Hearing her name made my heart sink. 'No, I... I was in the shop, just for t-two minutes, and when I came back, she... she was gone.'

'Okay,' said Detective Johnson, 'well, could you describe what April was wearing before she went missing?'

'Um...' I said, closing my eyes. 'A pink and white dress, with polka dots... pink shoes – pumps, I think – and she had a pink ribbon in her hair.' I started crying, remembering the little details of her. How could someone take my baby girl?

'Thank you,' said Detective Johnson, smiling gently.

I took her hands in mine. 'Please find my daughter, Detective,' I choked. 'I've already lost her father, I can't lose her too.'

'I promise you, my team and I are doing everything we can to find April. I'll be back later.' Detective Johnson left the room, closing the door softly behind her.

I lay back down on the couch, releasing my tears and letting them roll down my cheeks. I was only able to form one clear thought:

Please, whoever you are... please don't hurt my baby.

* * *

Hours passed, and there was still no news of April. Occasionally, an FBI agent would come in and ask if I was ok, if I wanted coffee, etc. Aside from that, I just continued to lie on the couch, trying to get rid of the empty, bottomless feeling in my gut.

Eventually, Detective Johnson came back. I immediately

sat up straight. 'Have you found her?'

'Afraid not, Miss Wood,' Detective Johnson said. I could see the dark circles underneath her deep brown eyes; she looked exhausted. 'You should go home and get some rest,' she added, 'I'll let you know if there's any news.'

'No, I can't go home,' I said, tears welling up in my eyes. 'It'll only remind me of her. I'll sleep here, it's alright.'

'If you're sure, ma'am. I'll get someone to get you a blanket and pillow.'

I whispered my thanks as Detective Johnson left the room.

The couch was extremely comfortable, but I still struggled to sleep. Every time I shut my eyes, I pictured her; on the swings in our backyard, playing with her Barbie dolls, munching happily on her bowl of Frosties. She was my world. The thought of losing her was too agonising to bear.

At 9am sharp, Detective Johnson came back into the room. 'Morning,' she said. 'How did you sleep?'

'Fine,' I lied. 'Any news?'

Detective Johnson shook her head in reply. She shifted back and forth on her heels. I sensed that something was up.

'What is it?' I asked.

'How would you feel about doing a press conference?' she asked. 'It's just that I think that it would really help the investigation – someone might know what happened to your daughter.'

I looked up at Detective Johnson. 'I'll do anything to get my daughter back.'

She smiled sympathetically. 'Of course. Follow me.'

* * *

The press conference room was quite small, so when the reporters and camera crew piled in, it felt like there were a hundred of them instead of twenty.

I swallowed hard and cleared my throat. I hated public speaking.

'My name is Claire Wood,' I said quietly. 'Yesterday morning, my seven-year-old girl, April... went missing. I went into the Salt Lake gas station to get a box of cereal, and when I got back into my car, April was gone.' Tears welled up in my eyes, so I tightened my grip on the picture of April in my hands to stop the tears from spilling over.

'April loves the colour pink, playing with her Barbie dolls, and swinging as hard as she can on the swing set in our backyard. She loves to have a bowl of Frosties in the morning, and she has to read a book every night otherwise she can't sleep.'

I cleared my throat again. 'I'm begging you, if you know where she is, please contact the police. She is a good girl, she would never hurt anyone.' My tears spilled over the picture of April, dampening the edges. 'Please bring her home to me. She's my everything. Thank you.'

* * *

It has been seven years since my baby girl went missing. There have been countless arrests made, but there has never been enough evidence to convict anyone with abducting April. I've given countless press conferences, radio interviews and TV appearances appealing for someone to come forward with information. Neighbours visit my house every day, asking me how I'm doing and offering their services. A memorial plaque was placed in Salt Lake Square, in memory of April. However, none of this will bring her back to me. The empty feeling in my gut has never gone away, and it never will.

I can never accept her disappearance. I can never move on with my life. I still go to the same gas station every month or so, and buy a new box of Frosties, just for her. And every day, I wander through the streets of Salt Lake, waiting for her to come back into my arms.

Snap!

By Kate Moore, aged 16.

'So. How are you?'

'You know how I am. We had breakfast together.'

'C, we didn't have breakfast. I had cereal; you left and came back with chips.'

'We ate together. You wouldn't make eye contact.' He was relaxed, that infuriating grin ever-present on his stupid face.

'Still doesn't count as breakfast. When you're not eating mass-manufactured cardboard-like products it doesn't count as breakfast.'

'You need to get better breakfasts.'

'You're wasting camera space.'

'You're wasting my time.'

I sighed. Carl was clearly loving this.

'Alright, C. Let's start again. Do you remember how we met?'

* * *

It is my firm and often-proven belief that public bathrooms of nightclubs exist, perhaps primarily, to provide refuge for bewildered journalists. I dashed in, manoeuvred myself into a cubicle, and immediately dropped my messenger bag, all its contents skittering across the floor. The evening so far had not been a success.

I got down on my hands and knees, scrambled for my belongings and inadvertently eavesdropped on the conversation going on behind me.

'Have you got them?' The voice was high, strung-out. Frenzied, even.

'Of course I have, French. When have I ever failed you? Shush, now.'

I shuffled around in the confined space, peering through the gap between the door and the slippy tiled floor at the two men by the sinks.

One was tall, with dark hair barely lapping at his neck, tapping his fingers against his thigh much quicker then was natural. Jittery – that was the word.

The second, the one facing my cubicle, was shorter, well-built, and pale-faced, with a shock of hair the colour of charcoal and kohl ringing his eyes.

'Carl-I-I'm not sure about this.'

'Look at me now, French.' Carl grasped French's shoulders. 'Would I ever lead you into a bad situation? I value you, my friend. We're mates, right? You can trust me.'

'But isn't it-'

'Illegal?' He began to rummage around in the pocket of his coat. 'Oh, yes. But not as long as you don't get caught.'

What on earth was going on?

Carl seemed to have found whatever he was looking for. French started as he retrieved something from his pocket. I strained my neck to see further. Great. I already look enough like a giraffe as it is.

It was a sort of packet, this thing. No, two packets, made of silvery cellophane. The man snapped something out of one. Something small, and round. I was pretty sure it wasn't vitamin C.

'You ready?'

'I-'

'Are you ready?' He said it with such force that the perennially nervous French clearly felt that he had no option but to agree.

'I-yeah.'

The black haired man offered his arm. French stood there, confused. The man rolled his eyes and linked his arm through French's, placing a tablet in his palm. 'Three, two, one!' They both took them at once, arms interlocked, bonded, somehow. There was a sort of grand theatricality to it that Carl obviously relished.

I didn't see French's reaction, but I did see his shoulders suddenly relax. I tried to breathe as quietly as possible.

'So...did you find anything?' This was Carl, again.

'Did I? Uh, yeah. She's here, alright.'

'That's not relevant, French.' His friendly tone was gone, and I could have sworn I could hear his heavy breathing from where I was.

'What do you want to know, again?'

Carl turned to face the mirror.

'I want to know why she's here. Whether it has anything to do with me, and whether she has what I want. And if you breathe a word of this to anyone-'

'Don't give me the stereotype rubbish. I get it.'

'Don't take this lightly, French.'

'You're still in love with her, aren't you?'

He stiffened. 'Shut up.'

'But you are!'

Carl turned to face French, grinding his teeth, mouth pressed into a thin line. He swallowed, fists clenched, shoulders heaving. You could practically feel the anger radiating from within him.

'Shut up! What do you think gives you the right, especially in this situation, to argue with me, to be anything other than unfathomably polite, in fact? Why do you think you can speak to me like that and get away with it?'

'But I- but you said we were friends!'

He approached French, head held high.

'Just how naive are you, Mr. French? Tell me that!' He was now nose to nose with the taller man, somehow seeming so much more impressive. He pressed his palms against the flat stone, trapping French between his arms.

French tried desperately to get away, moving when there was nowhere to go.

'Oh! What a shame. Scared, are we?' He spat the words out.

French screwed his eyes tight shut and seemed to be pretending this wasn't actually happening.

'I,' he said, pointedly, 'Am going to let you go now. But if you breathe a word, just a single word, of this to anyone, I will, and not in a Liam Neeson way, find you. Is that alright?'

'Yes! Yes!' gasped French. Carl stepped back, and French practically knocked him over in his efforts to get out the door.

Carl turned to the mirror for a moment, several moments, and then walked straight out the door.

* * *

'Tell 'em about your 'encounter' with Victory!'

'Victory hated me.'

'Still does. I asked her.'

* * *

I was here to interview a girl. Only one of the best, most talented, most generally amazing rock stars this planet.

Evidence from our paparazzi was always right, and evidence from our paparazzi showed that she was here tonight, at this after party.

She'd better be, or it wasn't worth it.

I'd seen Victory Wilson once already that night. She'd been on the red carpet, with some manager or other, looking either intoxicated or confused.

Our conversation had proceeded somewhat like this:

Me: 'Uh, excuse me, but are you Victory Wilson?'

Her: 'What?'

Me: 'Are you Victory Wilson?'

As if it wasn't obvious.

Her: 'You're an idiot.'

Successful by my standards.

The music was still blaring, but it was the time of night when an awful lot of people are trying to gather their significant others in order to get home. The thick air smelled of sweat and aftershave, and I had to fight my way through the crowds. Fighting to what? Was this worth it?

Someone had turned the lights down, so faces kept looming out at me from the gloom.

And then I spotted her.

I didn't know why I hadn't seen her earlier, frankly. She sort of stood out. Long, long red hair flowing around her waist, black dress twirling out around her feet, she was the only one dancing like that.

I mean, not like a dance. More like an attack.

Something was wrong.

I moved towards her, instinctively, so I was there when she fell. Tumbling, toppling from what to me seemed like a great height. She was so much taller than I was.

I was beside her when everyone moved back, spreading out like she was a fungus (instead of a genius). Some horrified, some excited, but no-one except me to actually catch her.

God, how was I going to get her off the dance floor without the paps coming flooding?

She fell over my shoulder, whilst I sort of tried to drag her, shielding my face and her own as the cameras flashed, snarling at them, elbowing my way through. I knew this business.

There was a door in the corner, and as we left the dance floor I heard a crash. Some other poor sod had experienced some sort of catastrophe. We reached the door alone.

I hauled it open a crack, realising with a jolt that it was heavier than she was. She was hideously light to carry.

It was then that I comprehended the voices.

'You'd better get out. Now. I have a feeling something's going to...happen.'

'You mean someone's called the police?'

It was the same two from earlier. I was surprised that Carl had stuck with French. They hadn't exactly struck me as friends.

'I don't know. But I got angry. And when I get angry, bad things happen.'

He really was just a walking stereotype.

It was at this stage that Victory Wilson chose to be sick all down her, and my, jacket in one swift coughing motion.

'Oh, thanks.' I hissed, though obviously she couldn't hear me, as the two men both turned to face me.

But, instead of the inevitable getting-my-head-kicked-in I had expected, Carl's face distorted in shock.

'What the hell did you do to her?'

53

He pulled the barely-conscious Victory away from me, glaring at me as if I'd done this myself. I did not want to get on this man's bad side.

'Do you know her?' An idea clicked in my brain. My interview...

He sat down, her head in his lap, and shook her. 'Victory! Are you OK? Are you alright?'

She blinked groggily. 'Carl?'

'What did you do?'

Was he her boyfriend or something? He'd be perfect for it. 'Nothing! Honestly! She just...collapsed! Is she OK?'

'No she's bloody not!'

'Look.' I knelt down beside them. French dithered in the background. 'I have a friend inside who's a doctor. He can help her, but only if you promise me something.'

He looked up, eyes full of hope.

'This sounds insane, but can I interview you?'

The hope turned to pure, undying hatred.

This was harsh, but the time for kindness was over. 'If you don't get her help, she'll die.'

'I'll do it. I'll do anything.'

That was the moment she recovered.

* * *

'And then she bloody wakes up.'

'Do you remember the first interview? C'mon, C, you've got to remember that!'

He rolled his eyes. 'Oh yeah. Now, that was a nightmare.'

* * *

Julian, my editor, had booked me a hotel room for the interview. As he slid the key into the lock, he muttered 'You'd better be right about this, Alex.'

I'd simply told him that I had someone to interview who was very close indeed with Victory Wilson.

That was a complete lie. I had no idea who this man was, other than that he was a prolific drug dealer, somehow knew one of the best rock stars of my generation and owed me one.

He was also probably horrendously unreliable with no sense of honesty in the least.

It was looking promising.

The room was big, more like a suite. There were two round chairs over by the window with a table in between, two chairs I deemed perfect. I sat, and waited.

It wasn't like I'd kept my side of the bargain anyway. Victory had been fine. She'd woken up, had a screaming match with Carl and stumbled away.

So, come to think of it, he really owed me nothing.

But he turned up anyway.

Edging nervously around the side of the door, Carl was dressed in dark jeans, a black t-shirt and jacket. He glared at me, unwashed streaks of hair falling into his eyes, came over, and fell into a chair. I had my questions all made out and ready.

'Ahem. Name?'

'Well, this is dull, isn't it?'

'Please, Mr O'Brien, co-operate.'

He sat forward. 'Tell me. If you already knew my name, why did you ask for it?'

'I just want an interview.'

'Why?'

'You gave me your word.'

'Which was given at the price of the safety of the person I love? And your side of the bargain was not upheld.'

'That's not relevant.'

'Oh, I rather think it is. Why the interview?'

'What is your relationship with Victory Wilson?'

He snorted, standing up. 'Oh, that's what this is. A silly little paparazzi interview by a silly little journalist intent on scoring his story. How nice for you. But you won't get it from me.'

'Are you her boyfriend?'

'When are you going to stop with the questions?'

'When you answer them.'

'Look, my friend. I might get angry soon, and you don't want to see that.'

I realised that there was only one way to get him to talk. So I did my best parrot impersonation.

'You're still in love with her, aren't you?'

'Oh. My. God.'

There was a silence. But the reaction this time was different to how it had been with French.

Carl's face whitened, like it had back in the alley. But this time, it was not ashen. More like snow.

What happened next, I could not comprehend.

He began to glow. His hands, his face, his ink-black hair, glowed white, white with a light brighter than the sun. I had to look away, shaking, my breathing disintegrated; I was choking, dying...

And then I woke up. I was on the footpath outside the hotel. Sitting there, wide-eyed, being stepped over by tourists.

There was somebody waving a hand in front of my face. I looked up. 'Victory?'

'Damn right it is. Come with me.'

This was all moving too fast. We weaved down through Grafton Street, night-time dawning.

'God, you look confused.' She laughed.

'I am.'

'Let me explain.' She mused. 'How best to say this? Well, Carl O'Brien has powers.'

'What?'

'He can make things happen, transport people, make people feel things that no human being should feel. He forms connections. He only knows that when he gets angry, or upset, things happen. He doesn't understand it, but I do.'

'Are you in a relationship?'

'Not exactly. Carl was my assignment.'

'Come again?'

'I belong to an agency, Alex. We find people with magical powers that they don't know how to use, and help them out. Unfortunately, Carl has been delayed. His have gone further than we've ever seen before.'

'And that means?'

'Oh, not much.' She said cheerfully. 'Just that he may be about to blow up the whole of Dublin.'

* * *

'Now she tells you. Timing!'

'She does like surprises.'

* * *

The venue for Carl's potential destruction of Ireland was a tiny pub in Temple Bar.

They had a list of famous Irish customers on their wall. Bono, Bressie, Colin Farrell...

Psychopath initiator of the destruction of the entire city and potentially country...

Just the usual, then.

There was a tiny table down the back with seven chairs. Two people were already seated.

Two large men, a woman, French, and Carl himself.

His eyes were ringed in black, his skin milk-white and he wore an unhinged grin that seemed to keep, unsettling, slipping down his face.

'Hello, Alexander! Lovely to see you. Absolutely charming!' his voice was different too. Slurred.

His hands were handcuffed behind his back.

I slipped cautiously into the seat opposite him.

'Alex,' Victory murmured. 'You, I, and Mr. French are the three who formed a connection with him. Only we can stop this. These,' she motioned to the others, 'are my colleagues.'

I gave them a quick nod. 'What do we have to do?'

'Play cards.'

'What?'

She shrugged. 'I didn't make up the rules. There was a wizard, and-'

'Seriously? The fate of the entire city depends on whether we can beat a drug dealer at cards?'

'Pretty much, yeah.'

'Which game?'

Carl butted in. 'You decide.'

I figured the night couldn't get more ridiculous. '"Snap'.'

'Why couldn't you choose something classier, like poker? I'm great at poker…' French trailed off as Victory shot him a look.

One of the men unlocked Carl's handcuffs, and he brought his hands up to the table. They were riddled with veins. His teeth were yellow. 'My deal.'

The irony. Not drugs, but cards.

And so he dealt. And we played. French was out in a heartbeat. Victory gave me a companionable nod.

It was surprisingly dull. The bar emptied out (not that there were many people in our area, anyway), Victory's associates went for drinks, French took constant trips to the loo.

Still we played. For anyone who doesn't know, the aim of Snap is for each player to place a card onto the pile in the middle until they get a match. If there's a match, you slam your hand down and yell 'snap!'

It's very simple, but surprisingly tense.

Victory played the king of clubs, her final card.

Carl placed a card on top of it.

'Snap!' he had the bundle.

She was out.

The fate of Ireland was relying on me, a party game and a deck of cards.

'You sure you can handle this, Alexander?'

'I'm sure.'

We both had roughly even piles of cards in our hands, but they swiftly dwindled down until we were left holding three solitary cards each.

Never had a game of Snap been so even.

He played an ace, I a four. He played a nine.

I played a nine.

My heart was in my mouth as my reflexes kicked in and my palm slammed onto the hard, polished oak.

'Snap!'

There was a roar, and Victory flung herself across the table at Carl. She and he, writhing beneath her, and the chair, all flipped backwards, tumbling across the tiled floor.

Her friends had come running.

But she no longer had to restrain him, he was out cold.

French emerged from the bathroom, wiping his sweaty palms on his trouser legs.

'What did I miss?'

* * *

'This is the fourth time we've done this interview, you realise? Julian is going to lose his-'

'Well, you never co-operate.' I cut him off before he could swear. I didn't need that on tape.

'At least you saved Dublin.'

'And Ireland. But that's weeks ago now. And it'd never have happened if it hadn't worked and your powers hadn't been drained.'

The camerawoman called to me from across the room.

'Alex? We're out of memory.'

I stood up, and went to hug Carl. 'See you same time next week, then?'

Until Death Do Us Part

By Saffron Dunne, aged 16.

I had gotten my third cup of coffee this morning and I could already hear May's voice, whispering in my ear; *stinky breath* before she would bury her lips in mine and tell me she loves me. That's one of the things that never grows old about May. She changes her mind like the weather but she loves me, I know she'll always be there by my side even when-

'Ryan! Hi, honey', squawked Nora. *Honey,* she never calls me *honey*. She's just one stuck up, nosey woman in my opinion. She had taken a seat on my desk and placed her paper cup of tea down next to my coffee cup. I had feared I would drink her cup instead of my own but the smear of red lipstick begged to differ. Nora was still there and I was carried away in my thoughts, as always. 'So, I see you're working?' she continued.

Well, that's clear, I thought as I looked up at my desktop of accounts. I could hear the busy, commutative sound of typing, tapping of pens and chatting amongst my colleagues and I had just realized that I hadn't said a word to a soul since I'd taken my seat. I smiled slightly at Nora, 'well, yes'. I'd felt like Nora had expected me to say more but I simply sipped my coffee and cleared my throat to break the tension. Luckily, Boss turned up so Nora went scrambling back down to her desk at the end of the room. 'Mmm, can I speak with you Ryan, in my office?' he said, more a demand than an offer.

My boss, Ted, was a short, plump man who was balding early enough. It was rumoured that he dabbles in *Charlie,* maybe more, from time to time. I followed him into his office and he shut the door after me. He looked at me when he took his seat behind his desk on one of those spinning-chairs and he gestured to the seat opposite his pudgy, little belly, 'please do', he said in his potentially high-pitched but chesty voice. I took my seat and looked Ted in the eye. If he wanted to fire me then I'd be fired with dignity.

'So, how're you doing?' he asked with a little smile, barely noticeable beneath his chubby cheeks that sat unevenly on his face. I felt confused. Had Ted invited me in for a chat? In that case, I should've brought my coffee.

'I'm well', I answered with a friendly, 'employee-of-the-year awardable smile', 'how about you?'

Ted frowned and sighed, looking down at his lap. Then, he placed his two hands on the table, gently. 'Look, I think you need to take some time off work. I think that would be better for all of us, wouldn't you agree, Ryan?'

I clenched my fists from under the table. *Is this Ted's way of off-ing his employees? Coward. He couldn't even say the words.*

I left the office at twelve o'clock that day. I'd barely started my shift and I was suddenly told to 'take some time off'. How convenient? All my mates were entering their shifts as I was leaving with my head down and fists still clenched. I had felt humiliated. I caught a glimpse of Nora. She waved at me and then bit her lip. I could tell that she didn't know what to say.

When I finally reached home, I noticed May's car wasn't in the driveway. *She's probably out shopping* I thought and headed inside the house. A grand house it is, big and warm and the peach-coloured paint on the walls glistens in the sun.

I tossed my set of keys down on the table by the front door before I paused. I could hear a ticking noise. *Drip-drop, drip-drop.* The bloody tap! I'd forgotten to fix it. I was heading into the kitchen when I felt a hand on my shoulder. It was May! Her soft, gentle touch melted my insides. I turned round and she smiled at me.

'May. I must tell you something. I-I was fired' I said, looking down. I felt embarrassed to admit it, 'well, Ted said I should take some time off so that's something, isn't it?'

I smiled and reached out to kiss her and she stepped back, almost startled or…repulsed? 'What is it, honey?' I asked.

'Where's Kate?' she asked, her eyebrows furrowed.

I half-shrugged before admitting 'she's with Jane'. I sighed and rubbed my face with my palm, 'apparently we're unfit to look after our own bloody daughter!'

'That silly sister of yours!' May said with a slight smile and crossed her arms. 'We must bring Kate back home, honey'.

I almost burst into laughter. Firstly because May was too kind to call my sister anything more than silly, which she was, and secondly because it was stupid thinking that we could get Kate back from the clutches of her pretentious aunt.

'She's our daughter, Ryan' May said in a shaky voice and I knew that she was about to cry. I hated to see women cry so I would agree to anything to stop it. 'I love you'.

With that I left the house, waving goodbye to my beautiful wife as I reversed out of the driveway. She looked upset and something seemed unnatural about her. I thought it was because Jane had Kate, so I drove away. I left her.

I reached Jane's house and parked my car across the road in case I would have to sneak into her house. There was a key under the mat and she wouldn't be expecting me, so that was an option, but she was home. I could hear her coughing as I waited at the door after ringing the doorbell. Jane opened the door, a cigarette between her left forefinger and index finger. She looked exhausted but managed a smile when she saw me.

'Come in!' she said warmly and shut the door after me.

'So…you're smoking around my daughter?' I tutted and took a seat on the ottoman in the living room.

'Stop it Ryan,' Jane said with a sigh and she rested her face on her palm, 'please don't'.

'What's up, Jane?' I asked, quickly checking my phone. May hadn't texted me all day. She usually texts me at around eleven o'clock in work as my shift starts at eight A.M. 'You look terrible'.

'And you don't!' she remarked. 'You just look like you've been up all night. Might I ask what's up with you?'

I chuckled, *what on earth was my crazy sister on about this time?* I thought. Jane looked me in the eye, she looked confused and angry.

'Hmm, maybe it's because you've taken my daughter!' I said and stood up.

'Leave her alone!' Jane said, defensively. 'She needs me. You're just making her feel worse! I-I'm sorry'

'What are you talking about?' I gasped, 'I'm her father and I love Kate. She needs to come home to May and I, to her parents. May has asked me to come here and bring our daughter back home'.

Jane covered her mouth with her two hands in shock. I continued to walk out the door and she didn't try to stop me.

I went upstairs and into the guest room where little Kate had her toys dispersed around her. She was sitting on her knees and she was playing with the dollhouse May had picked out for her for her fourth birthday. I stood at the doorway and watched Kate playing for a minute until she turned around and looked up at me. She looked upset, like she had been crying. Then I looked at the dollhouse. She wasn't playing with it but she had scribbled on the inside of the miniature house with her pencils and her toys had been flung around. She had pulled the heads off all her dolls. 'What have you done?' I said, startled by the mess before me. She looked down and started to cry, 'Hey, what's wrong?' I swooped down and picked her up, I gave her a big hug but she wouldn't stop crying. I carried her downstairs in my arms, her head rested against my chest. 'It's ok, sweetie. We're going home'.

I strapped Kate into her booster seat in the back of my car. 'I'm just going to say goodbye to Aunt Jane so I'll be back out in a minute'. I kissed her on the forehead and headed back into Jane's house.

'What have you done?!' I yelled, 'Kate is in bits. She's ruined all her toys and she's…crying. Why?'

Jane was sitting on the couch, her face in her hands. She stood up, startled by my entrance. 'Ryan. I…I-'

'No!' I shouted, 'You don't get to apologise. Not after whatever it is that you have done to Kate'.

Jane walked up to me and reached her arms toward me but I shoved her away. 'You will never see Kate again!' I said and turned to leave.

'Wait!' Jane said, gently and I turned back around. 'Ok, I get it! I will never see Kate again but can I at least say goodbye to her? Please, Ryan'.

I sighed and nodded. For Kate's sake, I would allow her to say goodbye to her Aunt. We went out to the car and Jane opened the backdoor, 'goodbye sweetie. I love you' she whispered. I gritted my teeth and watched Kate hug her tightly, she clung to her top and finally let Jane go when she told Kate that she had to go.

Jane began to walk inside but then she turned her head toward us, 'how about we go someplace special. Come on, Ryan!' Jane said, sounding like an eager child. Kate smiled. She finally stopped looking sad and I couldn't say no and upset her again.

'Fine!' I grumbled, still mad at Jane. *I'm doing this for Kate* I thought.

Jane walked up to me, 'I'll drive. You won't know the way' she whispered.

So, I let Jane drive us to this 'special place' she had mentioned. She was heading to outer-town and I hadn't bothered to ask her where we were going. She stopped the car outside the graveyard.

'Isn't this a little depressing?' I said but she said she wanted to visit one of our relatives. I figured it was our mother. Kate was very close to her granny.

We walked through the graveyard and Jane was taking a different route, toward the newer graves. *Where is she really going to?* I thought. Kate seemed to also know the way. Finally, we stopped walking and Jane and Kate respectively looked down at a gravestone. I followed their gaze and read the name. It read: *May C. Parker. Born February 4th, 1983. Died May 3rd, 2015.*

I fell to my knees, I couldn't believe. I couldn't register it. 'No, no, no, no…' I cried, 'It can't be true! Tell me this is fake! Tell me!'

Jane gently shook her head and hugged Kate while I sobbed on the cold tarmac, my nose was all snotty and my eyes were itching. I had wanted to be strong for Kate but I couldn't.

Jane drove us back to her house and gave me a hot cup of tea. I didn't touch a drop of it. I held Kate and we cried together while Jane explained everything to me. I had denied it all this time. I had denied my wife was dead for a week. I hadn't showed up to May's funeral having convinced myself that she was staying at her best friend's house. I had been told to 'take some time off my job' because my wife had recently died and I had gone straight back to work as if nothing had happened. My friends had been worried about me, even Nora felt sorry for me. Perhaps she had told Ted that I was back in work. Jane was minding Kate as she figured I would be very upset and she was looking after her, despite me thinking she was the worst Aunt imaginable. Poor Kate had wrecked all her toys in anger and sadness. Jane was exhausted as Kate would keep herself up all night crying and Jane vowed not to leave her alone for a second after the tantrum of wrecking all her toys. Jane feared my poor honey might even hurt herself and she was hoping I would feel better soon. What no one knew was that I was in complete denial about my wife being dead. No one dared mention it as they thought it would upset me, so they would try to take my mind off it.

The final question I asked was how my wife had died. Kate had gone to the bathroom. Jane held my hand in hers, 'May died in a car crash. She was driving recklessly but she hadn't consumed any alcohol. She was actually on her way to the shop to get a pint of milk. A pint of milk'. Jane paused and then went on, her eyes glistened, 'she was entering the motorway and a bus hit her car. She didn't check her blind spot'.

Now it all came back to me. The policeman had come to my house, his hat off, offering his condolences. I'd offered him a beverage but he had said he didn't want to stay long. 'It's about your wife, Mr. Parker,' he said. My ears were buzzing and I spaced out for the entire conversation. He was a young man, new enough to the police force. He had tried his best to make me understand the story but I was too in love to take any of it in. Before I knew it, Jane was hugging me, crying while I sat still. I didn't move an inch, I didn't say a word. She told me she would take care of Kate until I felt better.

'It still doesn't explain everything', I said, choking on my tears, 'I spoke with my wife earlier today. She was in my house and she said goodbye like it was the last time I would ever see her. Or was it the last time I saw her? Was that really her or was our last moment that morning when she plainly said 'bye' and to 'fix the tap in the kitchen when I got home'?

Jane blinked rapidly as Kate came back into the room. 'Am I going home now?' Kate asked, jumping on to Jane's lap.

Jane looked at me and then to Kate, 'I don't know' she said.

A Wrong Turn

By Lauren Bright, aged 17.

'It's twenty, right?' Michael asked. 'Right,' the guy answered slowly, cautious. Michael handed over the $20. 'Thanks' the guy responded, grabbing the money. His blue eyes swept the alley vigilantly before dropping the little plastic bag into Michael's palm. 'Bye,' Michael said, pocketing the bag. Whistling, he made his way to the corner. 'Did you get it?' John asked as he reached him. 'Chill, dude. Of course' Michael replied, handing him the bag. John opened it, causing some of the white powder to spill out. 'Careful. Don't waste it.' Michael exclaimed, hastily shutting the bag. 'There's plenty. Otherwise I wouldn't be sharing it with you' John stated. They laughed, anticipating the high that awaited them. 'Let's go get Toby and Lincoln.' John suggested. They crossed the street, avoiding an irate driver in a black Chevy. 'What time you gotta be home?' John inquired, pushing open the park gate. 'Who cares, man?' Michael cried giddily. An avenue of trees lined the path, russet leaves sparsely decorating the branches. The autumn breeze loosened a leaf as they passed, causing it to fall, twirling and pirouetting on a kamikaze mission to the multi-coloured carpet of leaves below. 'Lincoln's got smokes?' Michael asked, motioning to him across the street. 'He's got them' John assured, leading the way.

'What's up?' Lincoln called as they reached him.

'Not much, dude.' Michael said. They stood for a while, discussing the latest football game. 'Where's Toby?' Michael interrupted.

'He's acquiring our refreshments,' Lincoln answered, pointing down the street. Toby stood, deep in conversation with an older woman. The woman shook her head

vehemently and started to walk away. Toby caught her arm
and dropped something into her hand.

'He's gonna get caught,' John muttered.

'Relax. He's a pro at this,' Michael laughed. Five minutes
later Toby sauntered towards them, beers in hand. 'Nice
work' Michael complimented.

'A little more difficult than last time, but my natural
charisma won her over,' Toby replied.

Laughing, the friends made their way up the street
towards a vacant building. The wood creaked as the door
swung, echoing around the derelict house.

'This place is perfect, Linc. How'd you find it?' Michael
asked.

'A buddy told me about it. He used it a few years ago to
shoot up. Nobody ever bothers with it.' Lincoln explained.

'I can see why. It's a horror movie waiting to happen!'
John complained, brushing cobwebs from his face.

'Hey, dude you want out?' Michael snapped. The
tension escalated.

'That's not what I said.' John replied, walking up the
winding stairs. Reaching the top he turned to the others,
'Hurry up. I wanna get wasted!'

'Pity we got no girls here,' Toby mused.

'All in good time, my friend!' Michael reassured him,
crossing into the room. Paint hung from the wall in strips and
a fine layer of dust covered every surface. Flies buzzed around
in aimless circles as the boys sat on the ground. 'Pass me one,'
Michael ordered, gesturing to the beers in Toby's hands.
Toby passed him one warily, motioning for the others to join
them on the floor. Michael lifted the bottle to his lips and
chugged the dark liquid down in one gulp. The tension
dissipated as he let out a rumbling belch. Laughter ensued.
'Come on. Let's get this party started!' Michael shouted. The

boys' vision quickly became hazy as a cloud of smoke enmeshed them.

John started coughing violently, choking on air.

'You ok, J?' Lincoln asked, looking worried.

'Ya… all good.' He coughed.

'I've got bad stuff' Michael said, reaching into his pocket. He shook some of the powder onto his palm and passed the bag to Lincoln. They snorted the powder and started to laugh as the inevitable buzz zinged through their blood. 'Later… ' Michael sang dreamily as he sank to the floor.

Toby sat up, hand on his forehead to numb the ugly side effects of their 'party'. He shook his head slowly, trying to clear his foggy brain. 'Guys…wake up' he whispered, shaking John gently with his foot. John groaned and rolled onto his back.

'It feels like I have a jackhammer drilling a hole through my skull,' Lincoln complained, sitting up cautiously.

'That's the price,' Michael said cheerily, the combination of drugs, cigarettes and alcohol seemingly having no negative effects on him at all.

'How can you stand?' Toby asked.

Shrugging Michael responded, 'Maybe just used to it? Come on. Let's hit the road'. He leisurely made his way over to the door, looking back at his friends, 'If you guys can stand!' Grunting the boys stood up and staggered over to where Michael lounged. 'You guys here tomorrow?' he asked as he led the way down the creaking steps.

'One day at a time, dude. Besides I've got football practice. If I live through today,' Toby answered.

'We've got a game tomorrow,' John explained, nodding to Lincoln.

'Fine!' Michael retorted curtly. The rest of the descent was spent in silence, the echo of their boots thudding off the steps the only sound. Pushing open the door the friends halted, blinded by the glaring sun.

'Have fun tomorrow,' Toby said to Michael, shielding his eyes.

'I will. I'll ring Asha' he grinned, leaving.

'Michael!' John called. Michael stopped, bracing himself for the oncoming lecture. 'What?' he asked. 'Just… be careful. All this will eventually take its toll. Someone will get hurt.' John said.

Ignoring the stark truth Michael carried on.

The door swung open as Michael barrelled his way into his house. 'Michael?' a woman called, warily making her way towards him.

'Not now, Mum!' Michael complained, shouldering past her.

'There's dinner in the oven,' she said timidly.

'Not hungry,' he mumbled, going to his bedroom.

'We need to talk,' his mother replied, following him.

'No. We don't,' Michael said, slamming his door shut.

'Michael,' his mother tried again.

'Shut up and GO AWAY!' he yelled, grabbing his baseball. The sound of his mother's ragged sobs echoed through his door. He could picture her, standing there, tears flooding down her cheeks. The sobs decreased as she moved away from the door. Michael hurled the baseball at the wall, rubbing his head with his hands. All the shouting had made his headache worse, causing his eyesight to blur. Shakily he lay down, squinting out the light streaming from the cracked window. He resisted the urge to throw up, staring at the ceiling to focus. The restricting cage of pain ensnared his mind, causing him to reach for his bottle of sleeping pills. Taking one he immediately fell asleep.

An owl perched on the branch of a tree, out of place in the dazzlingly sun. The mourners, garbed in black, clung to each other, crying. An oldish man limped his way up to the plot, sniffling as he stared into the hole. The young man lying in the coffin was Michael, hair slicked back, still and suspended in time. The man reached down to pick up a handful of dirt, to throw it onto the coffin. 'I'm alive!' Michael screamed, squirming to escape his invisible bonds. No sound came out, the man oblivious to his pleas. 'DAD!' he screamed as the dirt cascaded towards him. It coated his face, filling his mouth, covering his eyes, blinding him.

Michael trembled as he woke. He forced himself to look around, to convince himself he hadn't been buried. Groggily, he reached for his phone. Sitting up he dialled Asha, pocketing his pills as he did.

'Hello?' she answered.

'Hey, babe, it's me. You free today?' Michael asked, grabbing his jacket. There was a pause.

'Same time, same place?' she questioned, wearily.

'Yup,' Michael answered, shrugging on his jacket.

'Should I bring anything?' Asha asked.

'Nah, I've got that covered. Just yourself,' Michael smiled. Ending the call he went to the kitchen. He grabbed a bottle of vodka and slipped it into a plastic bag, the flimsy material barely able to carry the weight.

'Michael…' his mother began, entering the room.

'What?' he replied, gruffly.

'Please don't do this!' she pleaded. Michael turned. Her greying hair was tied up in a bun and her frail arms were crossed protectively in front of her body.

'Don't do what?' Michael asked innocently crossing the room.

'Don't ruin your life just because he left. He left me Michael, not you.' she said. Michael stopped, tears welling up in his hazel eyes. His mother started to cry.

'This is not about him. Don't tell me how to run my life!' Michael barked, roughly wiping away the tears.

'I've got a bad feeling about this' his mother said, reaching for him. He bolted towards the front door, upturning a glass table in his haste. 'Michael Clarke…' his mother began, treading over the glass, 'Someone needs to teach you a lesson. You can't act like this.'

'Don't bother. I'm a lost cause,' Michael stated, fleeing the house.

'MICHAEL' she yelled after him.

Michael jogged down the street, dodging strangers and avoiding the questioning and frightened stares. The bottle bounced violently in the bag threatening to break. He pounded the streets, trying to forget the exchange with his mother. His mother's voice reverberated around his head. Michael shook his head, chest heaving. Rounding the corner he spied Asha's raven-coloured hair dancing in the wind. She glanced around nervously.

'Hey, beautiful!' Michael called.

'You had another fight,' Asha stated, 'It's got to stop'.

'I know,' Michael sighed, pushing his way into the house. Silently they made their way up the stairs. Michael pushed open the room door, swigging from the vodka bottle.

'Do you wanna talk about it? 'Asha asked, concerned. She moved closer to Michael.

'No. I just want to forget. Will you help me forget?' Michael implored, caressing her face.

Sighing, she took his hands in her own. 'Not this time, Michael. This behaviour is destructive. It can't continue.' She sensed the fury rising in him like a tidal wave as he ripped his hands from hers.

'Fine,' he said coldly, walking away.

'Baby, don't be like that,' she pleaded. Michael sat down moodily against the wall, drinking from the bottle. Asha went to Michael and knelt in front of him. 'We can stop this. There are other ways,' Asha said. Michael continued drinking, ignoring her. She sat down, leaning against the wall. Banging her head softly, she questioned, 'How'd we get here?'

'Well, we climbed up the stairs, pushed open the door…' Michael joked.

'I don't mean how we physically got here. I meant how did we *get* here…' Asha replied.

'I don't know,' Michael said reaching into his pocket. The light shone through the bottle, illuminating the pills.

'Michael. You know you're not supposed to take your prescription pills in the middle of the day. They're to help you sleep,' Asha exclaimed.

'I just want to sleep,' Michael stated plainly, unscrewing the lid. Asha kept quiet, knowing whatever she said would do no good, watching as Michael swallowed the pill with a mouthful of vodka.

The pain did not dissipate as Michael's eyelids fluttered open, resurfacing from the blackness. Groaning he sat up. 'Babe?' he asked sleepily. No one responded. Moaning he dragged his hand down his face. His eyes dropped to the floor. 'Asha?' he asked panicking, all trace of drugs evaporated. 'Oh, God!' Crimson blood pooled on the ground from her neck, a deep gash stretching across her skin. 'Asha!' Michael exclaimed, holding her neck to try to stop the bleeding. Staring at her face he realised her eyes were unseeing, skin white as snow. 'A…sha' Michael said slowly.

He started to shake. He realised his hands were coated in her blood. Shocked, he kissed her forehead quickly, recoiling from her cold skin. His eyes started to water. To stop the tears he wiped his eyes with the back of his hands, registering something glinting. He gasped. It was a knife, dripping with blood. 'No…' he said slowly.

Footsteps pounded up the steps, the door flung open. Michael looked around blinking.

'Michael Clarke!' an officer said, gun trained on him.

'I didn't…' Michael began, staring.

'Michael. You are being arrested. You do not have to say anything.' The cop commenced walking towards him.

'But…' Michael said.

'Anything you do or say may be used against you in a court of law' the officer continued, reaching for Michael's arms, forcing him to drop the knife. 'You have the right to an attorney. If you cannot afford an attorney, one will be appointed to you by the state' he carried on, dragging Michael to his feet.

'But…' Michael interrupted, confused. The other police officers made their way to the body as Michael was escorted to the door. 'Do you understand these rights as I have read them to you?' the officer finished. Time seemed to stand still as Michael took one final look at Asha. She was so still. Michael had no clue what happened. 'Destructive,' he heard her say in his head, her voice floating away like a kite without a string. 'Someone needs to teach you a lesson,' he recalled his mother staying. Silently he dropped his eyes to the floor, and trudged confused, but defeated out the door.

Blueberries

By Eadaoin Counihan, aged 17.

'I'll tell you a story- a story that's true
A little man died
And his belly was blue.'

'Really?' Gary asked eyes wide with wonder.

'Would I lie to you?'

'How did his belly go blue?' asked Gary

'I don't know, too many blueberries maybe.'

'No,' Gary peered at the small, vibrant blue culprits cupped in his hand.

'Just might be.'

'No, Grandad!' Gary weighed the chance of the berries colouring his belly, before scoffing down the lot.

* * *

Grandad, old by Gary's standards, and not too old, more middle-aged, by his own standards was a lively, talkative man. Grandad leaned in listening to a weathered man chat about fish markets. Like the man, Grandad was brown from a life lived outdoors and his wrinkles were deep from the sea spray's cut. Yet his eyes held a life machine-brainwashed youths lacked and young children blossomed with. Engrossed by the chat of the fish market picking up due to over eager tourists and health cults, Grandad failed to notice Gary slip into the stream of the bustling town market.

Gary dodged and ducked desperately as a wave of bodies pushed him forward and back. 'Fish, fresh fish', 'apples, onions, rhubarb, carrots', 'two for the price of one' and other persistent, ordering tones ambushed Gary's ears. Grandad, where was Grandad? People crashed against Gary. He stumbled knocking over chunks of slimy fish and handcraft candles. Cries soared high. Grandad! There he was. Gary rushed to get to the edge of the constantly moving crowd. Battling his way through Gary strained his eyes trying to pinpoint Grandad. Stumbling Gary broke free of the shoving clustering crowd.

'Grandad!' Gary ran to the man sitting low on a stone wall.

'Whoa, sonny, mind yourself!' the man steadied Gary. Gary stared silently. Before his very eyes stood a man, definitely a man, but he was just an inch or so taller than him. 'What is it, sonny?' the little man sat back up picking up a plastic container of blueberries.

'You're the little man!' Gary sat stunned on the grass.

'What, you've never seen a dwarf before, sonny?' the little man popped a juicy berry into his mouth, 'Like one?'

'My grandad told me about you,' Gary picked a fat berry.

'How do you know he means me, there are loads of dwarves?' the little man mused.

'The berries,' Gary explained.

'What did your grandad say?' the little man replaced the empty container with a new one brimming with berries. Gary recited the rhyme.

'Well, sonny, you've got me. I better cut out the blueberries,' the little man joked. Gary bit his lip. He didn't want the little man to die.

'Ah sonny, don't worry. Look!' the little man rolled up his t-shirt to reveal a swollen cut smeared with glistening foamy cream. 'Forgot about that,' muttered the little man.

'Did you fall?' Gary rolled up his shorts to display his grazed knees.

'Not exactly, sonny,' the little man chews his blueberries.

'Grandad says you should tell on bullies or they'll continue. They have to know you're not scared to speak out,' Gary rolled off his Grandad's wisdom.

'Why do you think I was bullied, sonny?' the little man stilled.

How did Gary know? It was all the little things his young mind couldn't place in words; the way the way the little man turned to hide his wound, his bending shoulders, and his darting eyes. 'You sound sad,' Gary settled.

'Sonny, that's fine in words, but not everyone is past the Middle Ages, they think I am a freak of nature,' the little man tried to explain.

'Because of all the blueberries you eat?' Gary wanted to understand.

'Because I'm short,' the little man chuckled.

'Did you not eat your veg?' Gary puzzled.

'I ate my veg, even the sprouts,' the little man sighed. 'Waste of my time. I never grew another inch.'

'Are they jealous?' Gary questioned.

'Jealous of what, not being able to reach jam on the highest shelf?' bitterly the little man commented.

'They can't not like you. They call me "little man" too and they like me,' Gary was exasperated.

'You'll grow,' the little man forced himself to relax.

'You can always roll downhill, win at hide and seek, fly on a swing, find lost things under the couch, and swim in the shallow end of a pool...' Gary trailed off as the little man stared at him. 'What?' Gary nervously peered around. The market had quieted down. The fresh bread now stale, the stagnant smell of fish lingered in the air and tourists munched on chips to warm themselves from the sea's biting breeze.

'You're right,' the little man let out a belly full of laughter. 'Sonny, you've opened my eyes.'

'Have you seen my grandad?' Gary remembered his mission.

'What does he look like?' the little man prompted further description.

'Like me. I think or it's I look like him!' Gary began a lengthy description.

'Is that him, sonny?' pointed the little man. There Grandad stood as if time escaped his notice still chatting to the weathered fisherman.

'Grandad!' Gary beamed, but hesitated. 'Stop eating the blueberries. You'll die' Gary advised.

'Sonny, I'll die a "little man" no matter when I die, today or years' time, I'm not going to start growing now. It's not the berries that'll kill me. One more couldn't hurt, could it?' temptingly the little man offered a berry.

'Bye,' Gary nodded bye and ran to his grandad.

'Let's go, little man,' Grandad smiled as Gary hugged him.

'You're getting tall,' the fisherman politely noted.

'I met the little man eating blueberries, but he said he'd die little even when he was old so he'd keep eating,' Gary rushed to share.

'Yes, yes, great imagination,' Grandad addressed the fisherman, 'Let's go.'

'Grandad, did you meet the little man?' Gary excitedly pestered.

'No, did you see Michael Finnighan?' Grandad's eyes glint with the light.

'No, who is he?' Gary was sheltered from the steady flow of evening strollers.

* * *

'There once was a man named Michael Finnighan
He grew whiskers on his chin again
The wind came along and blew them in again
Poor ould Michael Finnighan … began again.'

Burning Dollhouse

By Lauren Hannon, aged 16

It had been a lot of hard work and had taken ages but, in the end, it was worth the effort. She had finished school and was finally leaving the small town that she was trapped in for the last eighteen years. Three or four years ago, she used to think that she would never make it this far, but here she was.

She walked up the stairs to the room she had spent most of her childhood in. The room now almost empty. She noticed things that she wouldn't usually have noticed before. The dream-catcher she had used for a week, before throwing it on the floor beside her bed because her nightmares had gotten worse, was now one of the only things left behind. A dollhouse in the corner of the room caught her eye. She remembered the day she got the dollhouse and the day he broke it. She looked at each part of it. Broken doors. Broken windows. It was clear that whoever broke it really didn't care at all. She got down on the floor and tried to see if it could be put back together. Her hands began to shake as all the memories from her childhood came rushing back.

She remembered the day he left. She didn't remember everything. She seemed to always remember strange things, like what the weather was like that day, or what colour jumper she was wearing. She didn't remember why he left or why he was so angry that on his way out, he kicked her new dollhouse so hard, that it shattered before her eyes. She remembered how the sky had looked as he disappeared into the distance. It was on fire, like burnt orange with little specks of red and pink splattered horizontally across. The day he broke her dollhouse was the same day the fire started, and it continued to burn for ten years.

She remembered her thirteenth birthday. The fire was still burning, but that summer the fumes became so toxic, that she needed to escape. The escapes she chose made things even worse. 3 am walks with people she barely knew. Locked doors. Loud music. And screaming. So much screaming. They helped her for a while, but in the end, they just made the burns worse. She spent her days alone, burning alive with the fire he had started. The fire left her with scars that she would probably always be too ashamed to show.

'The taxi's outside,' her mother shouted from downstairs.

'I'll be down in a second,' she replied, as the memories began to fade from her mind.

She walked down the stairs, out the door, and hugged her mother goodbye. She took one last look at the house she grew up in. The broken dollhouse. Her eyes glanced up to her bedroom window. The sun reflected shades of yellow and orange through her window and that's when she knew that she had to leave. She wasn't leaving because she didn't love her mother. She loved her more than anything. She was leaving because she wanted to take control of what had controlled her for so long. She hoped that leaving would cause the fire to cool, the anger inside her to dissipate and the love she knew was there to return. She was leaving because she had made it this far, and for once in her life she knew that she could make it further, that she could go further, that she could be more.

It's A Small World

By Andrew Wood-Martin, aged 16

Past – 6th June, 1920.

Twenty-four-year-old Bertie fastened his harness tightly around his waist, as he took two steps closer to the huge sinkhole before him. He and his friends had created a new hobby, in which they would abseil down sinkholes to discover the mystical beauty within them. Most of the people they shared their hobby with backed away without even attempting it. 'It's just so dangerous!' they'd tell Bertie. 'Nonsense!' he'd reply; it's only dangerous if you go alone. He made it so that he would never abseil alone. Today, however, Bertie had decided to go alone. Gregory, a close friend of Bertie, who loved abseiling as much as he did, had to pull out at the last minute, and after spending all day preparing, Bertie thought it would be a waste just to abandon the 'mission'. And so he decided to break his one rule, on this fateful day.

He clipped his bright red helmet on top of his head and inserted his lucky gold pocket watch into his right pocket. His pocket watch had a slight dent in it, as it saved Bertie's life by deflecting a bullet for him in the First World War. A picture of Bertie and his wife, Scarlett, was in the watch's interior.

Bertie began his descent into the dark chasm beneath him. He couldn't contain his excitement. He slowly lowered himself down the hole. His feet dangled beneath him, as he tried to grip them firmly on to the upcoming crack in the wall. Here, he took a short break. His only source of light was a weak miniature flash-light, and it didn't enable him to see the sinkhole's floor. He then continued to descend the rock face. After 5 minutes of careful abseiling, Bertie had hit a rock underneath him. In his mind, he had reached the cave floor. However, when he turned on his torch, He understood he still had a long way to go. He had only landed on a ledge, and could not yet see the cave's floor. Bertie sat down, and took another rest from his climbing. The cave walls were wet, and to his right, Bertie could see a cluster of stalactites hanging from the underside of another ledge. His excitement to see what mysteries lied at the bottom intensified greatly.

After five minutes, Bertie continued his descent to the floor of the sinkhole. The only sounds he could hear were the cacophonous clicking of the bats, mixed with the hollow drips of the water dripping from the cave walls.

Eventually, he saw the bottom of the sinkhole. Not thinking rationally, he rushed quickly to get to the floor. After this foolish act, he was lucky he didn't snap the rope. After turning on his torch, he began to explore the cave.

Bertie found the most amazing things in the cave. He shone his torch all around, and found it hard to take in all the beauty that surrounded him. Stalactites as tall as small men, stumpy stalagmites that reminded him of his fat cousin Robert, and passages that lead to more caves that quite frightened Bertie.

When he mustered up the courage, he decided to go through one of the passages. He left marks at the entrance to make sure he knew how to get back to his rope. After journeying through the small cave for what seemed like half an hour, he found the most beautiful lake he had ever seen. It looked like something from a fairy tale. It was crystal clear, and as still as death. He strolled calmly around the body of water. What made him smile was the fact that there were no beer bottles, plastic bags, or any other signs of human life in the lake. It seemed to Bertie that no other human had visited it before, and therefore it had no name. 'It must have a name!' Bertie thought to himself. And so, he named it 'Lake Eerie', for the simple reason that, although it was probably the most beautiful thing he had ever seen, it emitted a spooky atmosphere that frightened Bertie somewhat.

After eating the small sandwiches in his backpack, made by his loving wife, while sitting by the lake shore, he decided it was time to go. On his way back, he wondered whether or not his friends would believe his story. He could imagine it now: 'A lake? Underground? You're pulling our leg Bert!'

When he returned to the bottom of the sinkhole, Bertie wasted no time in hooking himself up to the rope, so that he could climb out. But as he was almost half way to the top, he suddenly noticed he was falling to the ground. It all happened so quickly. Within no time, he had landed back where he started. On the damp cave floor. Still alive, but in sheer agony. He then fell unconscious.

When he woke up, he realised that he was now stranded helpless at the bottom of a 50ft sinkhole. Over the years, he tried everything to get back to the top. He once tried to climb up the sinkhole's walls. He knew that this was hopeless, as the cave walls were extremely wet and slippery. After two days, his flashlight's batteries had been wasted.

After one year of feasting on dead bats and drinking water dripping from the cave walls, Bertie was weak and sick. He realised that his friends didn't even attempt to come to rescue him. He died an angry and helpless man, at the bottom of a 50ft hole, with his golden pocket watch in his clenched fist.

Present.

It's 2015. Twenty-four-year-old Mark Mattson, an ace adventurer who loved exploring spooky natural wonders, came across a 50ft sinkhole in the middle of nowhere. This was right up his street. He ran home, packed his abseiling gear, and by dawn the next morning, he was back at the sinkhole. He secured his helmet firmly onto his head. He then attached his harness, placed his long-lasting LED flashlight on his head, and began to abseil down the monstrous sinkhole. It took him barely a few minutes to descend the 50ft beast.

Mark landed on the ground. He carefully detached himself from the rope and began to walk around. His LED flash-light lit up the cave to display its entirety. He could hear the quick scurry of the cockroaches. The cave smelt murky and damp. After walking in one direction for half an hour, he decided to turn around and walk back.

Bored and disappointed after not finding anything worth bragging about, Mark began to walk back to the rope. This was when he detected a small twinkle down a passage he hadn't come across before. He walked closer, and saw an amazing lake before him. This was certainly something worth bragging about! But where was that twinkle?

Just visible under a pile of bat faeces, he saw the bare bones of a left hand, clutching a gold pocket watch. Mark kicked away the remaining bat droppings to see a full skeleton sitting against a wall in front of him. He was amazed and scared at the same time. He was sure the pocket watch would make a fortune. Happily, he walked with his new antique back towards the rope. He opened it, and what he saw in the watch's interior stunned him completely, so much so that he had to sit down.

'I don't believe it,' Mark said, 'This man looks the image of me!'

It was uncanny. The man looked like a black and white replica of Mark, with shorter hair and much better posture. Beside Mark's doppelgänger was a beautiful woman that must have been his wife. 'She looks like my Great-Granny Scarlett...' he thought to himself. He barely knew the woman. She died when he was six. On the back of the pocket watch, there was a small piece of writing inscribed in the watch, barely legible, beside a dent:

'Property of Bertie Mattson.'

After a quick scan of his brain, he remembered Major Bertie Mattson, who served in the First World War. His great-grandfather. After he connected all of the dots, he understood everything.

'That's the dent that saved his life when he was shot in the war!' Mark thought to himself.

Mark also remembered asking Great-Granny Scarlett how Bertie died. The answer he lived with for many years was: 'No one knows. He went off on one of his adventures and was never heard of again.'

He could barely contain himself. He took the pocket watch, and sprinted back to the natural light. This was the most emotional, interesting discovery Mark had ever made! If only great-granny Scarlett was still alive. She would have loved to see that pocket watch again.

He reached the bottom of the hole, and went towards his rope, only to discover it wasn't there.

Hands

By Emma Holmes, aged 16

I never wanted a little sister anyway.

I unwillingly let my mother grip my hand with her own sweat drenched palms and clammy fingers. I gazed out of the window of our bottle green rusting Toyota and tried to block out the sound of her short sharp breaths, her grunts, moans and regular screams of intense pain.

She lay back stiffly in the passenger seat, her legs spread wide apart due to the excessive size of her stomach. My father's eyebrows crossed as he glared at the traffic ahead through his delicate glasses. His fingers drummed on the steering wheel anxiously and my eyes wandered to his wedding ring. It remained sparkling gold despite the many years they had been married.

As I sat in the labour ward drinking endless cups of tasteless coffee and watching endless streams of swollen woman hobbling past I vowed never to become pregnant.

Extreme as my viewpoint may have seemed, it wasn't debatable. Even upon first glance of my baby sister, cute as she may have been, I did not take to her.

'She suffered a post-partum haemorrhage,' my father repeated to me.

'Yeah, yeah, loss of blood,' I knew all too well.

'Don't worry she's a tough cookie, your mum.'

I glared at my father as he nursed a tiny bundle of white cloth, I assumed that a child was swaddled somewhere in there, or else why he would have been smiling ridiculously at cotton sheets? How could he be so loving towards it? It had nearly killed my mum.

In the weeks after the birth, my father and I visited my mum often in hospital. She seemed paler each week and soon appeared as white as the bedclothes on her lap.

My father did his best with Lily – that was her name. He changed diapers and stayed up all night when he had to. And when my mother was fit to come home I wasn't given any choice.

'Your mother is poorly and needs her rest,' my father spoke to me like his skivvy, not his first-born daughter.

'Lily will sleep in your room, and you must take some responsibility for your younger sister.'

I could have spewed my anger at him in a ferocious bursts of insults but I loved my mother dearly and chose not to.

And if I could go back now I would.

I lay awake at first; fearful she would not fall asleep. And at first her sobs and cries startled me from my bed. But then I lay awake, in fear that *I* might fall asleep.

A scream sounded so horrid that it pierced my ears and resounded through my head. In the darkness I stumbled to the crib where she lay. Her tiny eyes were tightly closed and I listened to her shallow breaths in the silence. I waited to hear my father's loud footsteps across the creaking floorboards of our hall. But I heard nothing. I sat upright in my bed for countless hours, my hands sweating and my heart pounding.

The silence was deafening.

Each night it scared me more. The piercing screams. The pained cries. But yet a peaceful baby lay in the snow white crib. I clapped my ears to stop the incessant noise, yet my hands shook vigorously against my head, and the screams rang out loud. My parents were sound sleepers perhaps selective in rising from bed at times. Surely they must have heard this each night?

'The circles under your eyes have grown terribly pronounced'

As I poked through my soggy cornflakes with a rusting spoon I lifted my head to look at my father. He was stroking his now almost completely grey beard across his face as he read the Sunday Newspaper.

'Well, I cannot sleep at night.'

'It's certainly not because of your sister, anyway, she's as good as gold,' he smiled in the direction of the Moses basket in which she lay, having yet another peaceful snooze.

'She screams all night long!'

'As if I wouldn't hear that!' he scoffed loudly slurping a mug of coffee. He laughed at me like I was being ridiculous. My finger wrapped tightly around my spoon. I could have thrown it at him, or better still, scooped his beady eyes out with it.

But I swallowed hard.

'You choose not to hear her.'

'I choose not to hear you and your desperate attempts to get rid of Lily.'

Silence filled the kitchen. Then he mumbled, 'I am not the fool you think I am.'

My stomach knotted as I thought of the night ahead and I pushed the cornflakes across the table. I am no fool either.

I sat on my bed, my legs crossed. 10:30PM, by now my ears are usually filled with deafening screeches and my mind is filled with terror. However I am calm. 11:00PM, what is she waiting for?

11:27PM, the break of the deathly silence made my heart pound fast. But I was ready. My knees were weak. Possibly due to lack of food or sleep, or maybe I was doubting myself. My hands shook yet held firm. I made my way towards her crib. Over the bars. Covering her face. I placed it. A pillow. Screams roared loud in my ears and I shut my eyes tight. Pressing down in defiance, I screamed back. It was thrilling. My noise drowned out hers. I screamed out to stop. Screamed I had won. Screamed till it hurt.

Large hands gripped my shoulders. Firm hands threw me to the floor. Gentle hands feed my pills. Firm hands held me down. Yet no hands came to visit.

'Schizophrenia,' they say,

'Psychopath.'

'Murderer...'

My Best Friend Gave Me the Gun

By Paul Sweeney, aged 17.

I hear his voice again, hollow and resonant. Memories I had tried to obliterate into a vast expanse of nothingness have begun to materialise in every waking corner of my ravaged mind. I had thought it was over. Why am I still in anguish? The mere thought of him fills me with expectation of perpetual pain, physically and emotionally. I open my eyes to an ample view of a starry night sky. It is a damp night with hints of wintry conditions. I realise that I am lying down on a grassy clearing. But, why am I lying down? In my confusion, I just about remember what had stirred me from my lethargic slumber. I begin to swell up with panic again as I search for the source of the voice. Then I spot him; In the midst of police cars and an ambulance. But that doesn't even concern me at this moment. He's sitting on the hood of a police car, shoulders encased in what looks like a rugged blanked. But, something seems different. It's hard to see from here, but it looks like he's crying! Surely not. Six foot four Daryl Woodlock is hunched over whimpering. I had almost convinced myself that I was wrong, as it is hard to see him in the light of the dim headlights. I heard him sobbing even louder, almost screaming. A few heads turned to look at this broken teenager as his mother rushes over to comfort him. I have only seen his mother a few times, when she would pick him up from what she thought was after-school studying, but was really just him sticking around to torment me, after hours. She always seemed to be quite a shy and anxious person. She, of course, never found out though. I start to wonder why I haven't been spotted lying out in the clearing, but I suppose it is very dark and I am a good distance away. As to why I am even out here in this clearing under a huge cliff, I have no idea. I must have followed Daryl to end further risk of being spotted, I get up and hide behind a group of trees. I gaze at Daryl again and begin to contemplate what it is that he is crying about. In order not to drown in a pool of my own confusion, I decided to hide behind some bushes right next to the crowd of police cars. But, whilst running to my new hiding spot, I noticed that one of the police officers looked right at me, but at the same time, didn't seem to acknowledge me. This arouses my curiosity, but it quickly shifts onto the huge wreckage of a car in the midpoint of the police cars. I feel a rush of pity for Daryl as I realise that mangled body in the front seat of the wreckage must be someone close to him. Maybe a relative or even Jack or Neven, whom you might call his sidekicks. But this pity quickly washes away when I remember all that he has done to ruin my life.

It all started when we were in primary school. We were best friends, inseparable. Well, at least at school anyway. You see, Daryl was quite shy and secretive. We only ever saw each other at school. I invited him to my house on many occasions, but he always said no. If asked why he would always say that he 'wasn't allowed'. But he never elaborated on that. I didn't even know where he lived. I asked my parents and they didn't know either. The day our friendship ended was the day we both started secondary school. I walked up to him in the hallway and said 'Hey Daryl, I haven't seen you all summer'. He turned around and punched me in the face. I woke up in the hospital with a broken eye socket, and let me tell you, that is excruciating. I was filled with confusion, and it was not how he was able to break my eye socket with one punch, it was why he did. Since then, not a day has gone by where he has not inflicted pain and misery on me. Apparently the other students got the wrong idea about why he hit me, as if he had a reason, and cheered him on. I ended up with no friends, social anxiety and a slight nervous twitch if anyone spoke to me, or even looked at me. I have been through it all; punching, kicking, head down the toilet, being thrown in a wheelie bin and the being wheeled. I have gotten enough bruises over the years to cover my entire body. I have been unceasingly depressed for years. I have taken every antidepressant drug known to man and I even nearly over-dosed two years ago. But nothing works as the cause is always there. Depression is a disease. The worst possible. It will eat away at your brain until there is nothing left but sadness and morbid thoughts. It's worse than cancer as it doesn't kill you, it makes you do it. Instead of firing the gun, it puts it in your hand. There is no escape. In recent years it has lead me to alcohol. I can't go to school sober. The hangover is nothing compared to what I will feel there. I can't fight back, Daryl is twice my size, plus he has friends to back him up. I have nobody. There is no chance that I will tell my parents. Although, they do have their suspicions. This makes it worse. There is no greater agony than bearing an untold story inside you. Most of the time I am so quiet that people forget I am suffering.

A police officer has come over to Daryl. He says 'You were seen abusing the victim physically and verbally by several witnesses earlier this evening outside your school grounds.'

Daryl replies, in between sobs, something that sounded like, 'It's all my fault!' I couldn't hear much more of the conversation and eventually Daryl's mother said, 'Come on, the boy has been through enough.' Then Daryl and his mother trudged away. Their car doesn't seem to be here, so their house must be within walking distance. But I realise that I recognise this place. Stanley's Cliff. I remember running away from Daryl one day and hiding here. Since I, of course, don't want to see Daryl's suffering come to an end, I follow him and his mother home, making sure to stay in the shadows and not be seen. The house that they go into is small and unkempt. Daryl always told me that his dad was a lawyer so I'm surprised that that they don't have a better place than this. As I approach the house, I hear glass smashing and a scream. I hop the fence and dash over to the kitchen window. When I look inside, Daryl is on the floor, covered in shards of glass. His father is standing over him, his eyes filled with rage. His father punches him and continues to do so whilst his wife screams and pleads with him to stop. Daryl's father throws her against the opposite wall and starts to threaten her. He is obviously very drunk. This looks like it is a regular occurrence. As he pins his wife against the wall and he reaches for the kitchen knife, tears streaming down his wife's face. He lashes out. But Daryl, filled with desperation, tackles him. His father hits his head off the counter-top and doesn't look conscious. But there is blood everywhere. Why is there so much blood? I am in a state of shock and panic, but I'm frozen still as I watch Daryl's lifeless body hit the floor with a thump, blade still lodged inside. Daryl is dead. I look for my phone so I can call the police, but I cannot find it. I look up and see that Daryl's mother is on her hands and knees in the blood, wailing. I don't know what to do. All I can do is run. Run home. Run to my parents. It is pitch dark and every molecule of my body is crushed with despair, but somehow I make it home. I burst through the front door and into the sitting room where I see … myself? In a coffin. But I am barely recognisable. My family is standing around my coffin. Then, I remember. It all floods back and I feel like I'm drowning. After school, Daryl was worse than ever. In front of the whole school. Harsher insults. Fiercer punches. He looked around at all the horrified faces of the people watching and whispered to himself, 'I'm just like Dad!' then ran off. I went home. I was more depressed than I have ever been. I couldn't handle it. My parents weren't home. I swiped a bottle of whiskey from Dad's cabinet. I got in my car and just drove. I just kept driving and driving and driving until, nothing. I felt nothing. I didn't feel good. I didn't feel bad. I just felt nothing. Depression forced the gun into my hand once again and I finally gave way. I was nothing for what felt like forever, but could have been one second. I look around, at my family, at my wailing mother. I feel ashamed. I took a long term solution for a short term problem. My feeling of un-ending suffering has returned. Maybe the only way out is to forgive. I look to my right, I see Daryl. 'I'm sorry,' he says. I reply with, 'I forgive you.'

Nothing.

After the War

By Alana Mahon O'Neill, aged 17.

The allies had won and a peace treaty was signed, but when backs were turned, the enemy succeeded in their retaliation and I found myself captured and without trial imprisoned in the pillow fort with a plastic sword held in the crook of my arm.

'You can't move.' Captain Jack Sparrow sneered as I began to fidget with discomfort. My fellow Captor, Cillian, was anxiously removing a chocolate stain from his grey shirt with a wet wipe. He did not like dirt. His Mammy always ironed his clothes and combed his red hair with a perfect split down the centre of his head. He was a useless comrade. He could not even play dead. His wooden sword with the misspelled ESKALIBUR printed along the splintered blade in a green sharpie was thrown to his side.

The stain was his main concern.

'You are WOUNDED!' Captain Jack Sparrow, aka my younger sister Kylie hissed, 'You're meant to be DEAD!'

'You're a traitor.' I stated. Kylie was once begrudgingly with us, but that was before we were overcome and then she had quite happily changed sides.

'Blue Team…RULES!' She yelled triumphantly, waving a stunted flag she fashioned out of a blue dishcloth sellotaped to a wooden spoon.

I had never seen anything more despicable.

As she was distracted with her festivities, I used my time wisely to counter attack. I removed the sword from my armpit and walloped it off her shoulder. She fell onto her backside. She was for a few seconds rendered in shock before beginning to sob hysterically.

'THAT'S NOT FAIR.' She wailed, 'I'M TELLING MAMMY.'

As I made out the door she tried whacking me with the broken flag; a deadly wooden spoon with spikes of hardened sellotape. I was being fired at. What could I do?

I grabbed a handful of her hair and she screeched.

I glanced at my comrade who had not looked up during the entire episode and was still concerned with his stain. As a human being I had to persevere. I knew there came a time in life when one had to make a difficult decision to live and often at the cost of the life's of others.

But I really hated Cillian.

I dearly missed Robert; he was a valuable contribution to the Allied Red Team.

He unfortunately was called to a better place.

His Mammy was bringing him to McDonalds.

Death had taken another young soul too early.

Cillian being Cillian, Robert eating a Happy Meal and Kylie turning on us for the other team, I was sorely outnumbered. I had narrowly avoided death at the hands of the enemy, and now, I was in their grounds and desperately isolated. I know no man gets left behind, but Cillian isn't a man. Cillian isn't anything. Kylie sat on the ground and began to cry and all Cillian did was spit on his stain.

He made a wise choice.

The thrill of freedom and excitement rushed through my veins as adrenalin as I ran for cover beneath the trees. Yet I had to force a coolness to descend upon on my mind. It would only be a matter of time before somebody came by or Kylie got up and told on me. I did not want anybody to find me then. After all: we had gotten Cillian's Mammy and Daddy to sort out the fight me and Andy had earlier. We were meant to be finished before Cillian and I were forced into captivity. When they had retaliated, the peace treaty had been violated.

I am an ex-prisoner of war.

Oh, of course: we are at war, once again.

'Kylie, you okay?'

It was Jacqueline, Kylie's inseparable and completely insufferable best friend. They went around, arm in arm, high and mighty, for no apparent reason I could fathom, as they were both rather unappealing.

'Alex hit me.' Kylie squealed.

I remained stock still beneath the bush. Nobody knew of the hiding place and I did not exactly want to come out, anyway. Jacqueline was going to tell Cillian's Mammy and then she would tell my Mammy. And that would be the end of the world as I knew it. Yes, I could hide until Mammy came shrieking for me; tearing up trees and rocks to find me like an unstoppable tsunami. It could be done. I could put off my eventual capture as long as I could, or-

I could RETALIATE!

I was out before they knew what hit them. I grabbed Jacqueline's beloved hair clip from her long blonde hair and made for the opposite side of the clearing to the other trees.

'HEY!' she roared at me, tears ran down her face, as I had not-so-accidentally pulled out a lump from her skull, 'THAT HURT!'

Her first casualty of war: a lost butterfly clip.

It was a sad day for the sad person that was Jacqueline.

I said a prayer to God to play for her the world's smallest violin.

I ascended the tree and placed it in the hollow place between two branches. Now, it was Mother Nature's. I could bargain my way out of this. Kylie telling on me was the equivalent of spending the rest of my life with prosthetic legs. Then again, if Mammy knew I had hurt Jacqueline then she'd send me home in a body bag.

It was risky, but it was done-what choice did I have?

'If you tell on me, then you won't get your clip back.' I snapped.

'I'M TELLING MAMMY, ALEX!' Kylie wailed, 'Stop being mean-! I'm sick of you being mean! It's not fair! You're not playing properly! You hurt my hair! I'M GOING TO TELL MAMMY AND THEN YOU'LL BE SORRY! YOU'LL BE SORRY-!'

I did not stay to listen.

They knew I had my bargaining tool. Jacqueline would not tell on me as I would not give her back the clip otherwise. Kylie, no matter what, would not tell on me because then Jacqueline wouldn't get her clip back. They were two best peas-in-a-pod and absolutely perfect, weren't they? I would be a MONSTER for coming between such a poster-perfect friendship!

My main objective was the treasure; the ultimate achievement of the victor. What should have been my prize before Blue Team robbed us when our backs were turned. With the knowledge of the retaliation, I felt foolish; how could have I been so naïve and not see through deception?

As I was running between the trees of Cillian's ornate and elaborate garden adjacent to his lavish house, I was overcome by a foot that connected with my shin. It tripped and wounded me in the process. An overwhelming pain grew in my lower leg and I was unable to move on the ground. I looked and saw to my horror just how the kick from Jordan's Soccer Boots had left a shallow gash on my skin which had peeled back somewhat. It was probably not a very impressive or grand wound but I felt, all the more, overcome by it.

'Stop messing!' Jordan stood over me, his hands on his hips. He and Billy were Andy's henchmen. I was not afraid of Jordan or of Billy but I wanted to avoid Andy at all costs.

'I'm not on Red Team anymore.' I lied, 'I'm on Blue Team now. We're getting Cillian.'

'Really...?'

'Yeah...'

I feel that if this was actually happening then only trouble would result and Cillian's Mammy would never let us over again. I mean, I hated Cillian, but I loved his cool garden. Where else could I possibly hide a clip that would never be found, unless I was tortured? Though, then again I don't think I could succumb to pain and pressure, unless it was from my Mammy, herself.

I ignored the pain in my leg and stood.

'Yeah, as a matter of fact, I think you're a bit of Cillian.'

I gave him a master ninja-punch or at least something akin to it. I shoved him against the tree. It was harder than I expected and he made a whacking noise. He didn't cry like Kylie or Jacqueline but his face went bright red and his eyes shone.

He was about to open his mouth when a voice as menacing as a wolf's, as deep as a giant, as a cold as ice sounded through the trees-

'ALLLEEEXXX...!'

Damn. My Mother.

'LIIINNNDDDAAA...!' Jacqueline sounded, in return.

I needed to run. I left Jordan where he was. Instead of following me or shouting for Mammy, he got up and went towards the voice of the oncoming BEAST.

'Not too far now...!' I encouraged myself. It was a straight path to the kitchen. The wound on my knee was graver than I had originally assumed. A trickle of blood ran down to my ankle.

Oh God. I would have to amputate it now.

The kitchen. On the shelf was Cillian's Mammy's sewing kit. Perched on it was the jam jar.

Sacred wonders lay within.

'I knew you'd be here.' A voice said behind me.

Andy, my older brother, and flanked by the monstrously sized Billy who stared at me dumbly as I reached for the broom.

'What do you think you're going to do with that?' Andy raised his long finger and poked me hard and square in the chest, 'You're too weak. You're just a six-year-old. And a girl.'

Discrimination against the youth.

Misogyny.

War is inevitable in this cruel, patriarchal society.

I raised the broom and with the brush side, hit him around the head. I did the same to Billy, too. From experience, it was not nice being hit with dirty strands that had been on the ground.

'BIIILLLYYY…!'

Billy's mother. The BEASTS were accumulating. Time was closing in.

Billy sniffed miserably and ran away. He made heavy footsteps out the door.

Andy raised a disgusted finger at me.

'That's mine!' he hissed.

Too late.

I swung the broom and the sewing box and jar went flying from the shelf. Andy winced as the sewing box fell with a huge clatter and bang. Needles, thread and beautifully ornate cloths were thrown across the already immaculate floor. Although, in the eyes of Cillian's family, it was the equivalent of stewing the flag of their family crest in a pot of pig filth.

I caught the jar. Perfectly calculated.

'ALEX!' Andy lunged at me but I threw the broom and he fell over that.

I opened the jar.

Mammy's thunderous footstep on the wooden porch.

'YOU WOULDN'T…!' Andy gasped, his mouth agape.

The Allies were Victorious.

I feared no consequence.

I had achieved my bounty.

I removed the Kit-Kat.

I ate the chocolaty goodness.

It felt good.

Outside the Comfort Zone

By Ce'Nedra Cullen-O'Brien, aged 17.

Tightening his grip on the collar of his now saturated coat, he shivered. The strength of the rain hammering down around him had made his trousers stick to his legs like glue, and it was not a pleasant experience. James McDyre had been waiting in this side-street for near three quarters of an hour now and the rain hadn't gotten any lighter. He was lurking at the corner of a dark alley-way between an abandoned tenant building and an old theatre in the centre of the city. This was where he was told to wait. He glanced at the clock-tower of the old church across the street, just barely making out the hands through the curtain of rain, he noted the time; nine twenty five. She should be here soon. Slinking back a little farther into the alley to gain what more shelter from the rain as he could, James reached into his pocket and took out a small photograph. The edges were softened with age and the colour long-since faded, but the sight of it still made him smile slightly.

It was a photo taken three years prior of the woman he loved, her sand coloured fair hair and soft facial features as perfect as ever, her bright eyes and smiling face shone through the photo at him and calmed him somewhat. Placing the photo carefully back in the inside pocket of his coat he clenched his jaw. That night James had been meant to be with his love, it was the night he had intended to propose marriage to her. Brushing his hand over his left leg he could make out the shape of the box his carefully chosen ring was in. Being reminded of this made him curse with frustration under his breath. He knew she had understood, but at the same time he couldn't forgive himself for having to leave their date so suddenly. He took a glance at the clock-tower once more before returning his gaze to watching the street silently. James was hoping this was going to be worth it. Of all nights for him to be called in, it typically had to have been this one. In the distance he could see the vague outline of a car's headlights and squinted to be sure.

Yes. This was it, he was certain. He observed as the long car pulled up outside the main entrance and the hazy glow from inside illuminated the side of the car. A smartly-dressed door-man stepped out from beneath the canopy over the entrance to greet the car with an umbrella. James watched holding his breath in silent anticipation as the car door was opened and out stepped his target. He mentally took note of her build to prepare himself for the task ahead. The woman moved with ease and a natural grace. She smiled at the man holding the umbrella for her and lifted the bottom of her dress. Lifting it was wise of her, as there were puddles between her and the red carpet which was to lead her inside. The dress was a striking crimson red and it matched the thin red ribbon she had tied decoratively through her mass of dark curls that were cascading around her shoulders. Taking in any way aspect of her movement which could be to his advantage later, James watched her.

He looked on until she was roughly half way up the worn red carpet to the front door, knowing she would disappear out of sight when she reached the entrance. Seemingly satisfied with his observation he turned quickly on his heel and trudged back down the alley. His shoes sloshed through the deep puddles as he continued in the dark and he swore under his breath. James was wearing his dress shoes he had chosen for dinner and could feel the water seeping through his socks. Placing his hand carefully on the rough theatre wall he proceeded and felt along it taking care as he searched. He knew it was here somewhere... There! He felt the sharp edge of rusted metal when his hand came into contact with the door frame. Sliding his hand down the side of the frame he felt for the catch he'd checked was there earlier. Reaching it he kept his right hand over the catch whilst kneeling to take the hook from his ankle brace to unlock the door. He would only have one shot at getting it right so he had to be careful.

Sliding the small curved metal bar up under the nail he tilted the catch to the side slightly and pulled. Nothing happened. He began to panic but took a deep breath and moved it slightly to the right instead, being careful not to move it out of place. If he pulled the hook out now it would snap and be left stuck inside, that was not what he needed. Being careful to move it gently, James slid the bar to the side and held the catch in place with his thumb before giving it a firm tug. He heard the small 'Click!' and let out a sigh of relief, but not for long, now he had to move, it was all down to timing. Discarding the now useless and bent hook he grasped the door's metal bar with both his hands and pushed it down slowly. James wasn't sure what was going to be on the other side, this was the first time he'd been on a job alone and was used to the security of having someone beside him to back him up.

With one deep breath he pushed on the door and it swung open with a grinding sound of rusted metal being dragged against the inside door frame. Heat hit the man's face instantly and he coughed for a moment trying to get a grasp on his bearings once more. Startled and glancing cautiously around the inside room he was relieved to find no-one there. He stepped over the threshold, glad to be out from under the endless shower of rain. At least he was inside, although he felt uncomfortable in the heat of the small compact room. After closing the door behind him, James shook out his trousers and coat for a moment before trying to search for either another door or a light switch. He knew this was a boiler room, that's what he had been told it would be in his instructions, but he didn't know how to get access to the rest of the theatre through here, he was merely given the way in. Stumbling around in the dark of the boiler room he noticed a line of light along the ground to his right. It was coming from beneath a door, at last.

Approaching the door James froze, He could hear voices. Usually in this situation he would have more confidence that if he wasn't able to make it very far, that his accomplice at least could finish the job. It was all down to him this time, he couldn't afford any mistakes. Discovering that the door had an ordinary design of lock, he pressed his ear to the keyhole and held in his breath closing his eyes for concentration. 'Yeah Tony jus' came by 'ere, 'appy as eva', y'know 'im, always one for a cha'' James could hear a man with an accented voice say, followed by laughter. It was evident that whoever this 'Tony' was, he wasn't known for being one of good humour, at least according to whoever waited on the other side of the door. Then came a more smooth voice 'Well that's good, at least he's not watching the kitchens, What do you say we-' he coughed '-go have a bit of a potter 'round the pantry, eh..?' the voice was suggestive.

James listened, now hoping he may not have to deal with either of these characters if they did in fact go through with the smooth voiced one's plan. The accented man replied after a moment of apparent thought 'Silas, y'know we 'ave a job t'be doin', don' think we should be doin' tha' t'nigh'' the smooth voiced man – now known to have the name 'Silas' – moaned 'Oh come, *on*' (Silas stressed the 'on') 'don't be such a bore, you're worse than your sister sometimes' he said and chuckled to himself before coughing again. 'Oof! What was-?!' Silas was cut off. 'Don' be talkin' abou' me sister like tha', jus' shut up 'n let's go' muttered the accented man now sounding out of sorts. James listened intently for more conversation, but only heard their footsteps walking away and Silas' various complaints about how his shoulder hurt. Being now sure that the coast was clear James inspected the door. It seemed straight-forward, and from what he could tell it wasn't locked.

He took a deep breath and opened it out into the brightly lit hall. James was tense and cringed for a moment, expecting it to have been too easy and for an alarm to go off at any given moment. No alarm came, and he relaxed, before scouting out the halls with his eyes. There were two inter-connecting halls that met just beside where his door had brought him. Scoping out both halls momentarily he chose to go straight ahead as there was a blind corner at the end of the other optional hallway. Stalking up the hall he noticed both how quiet it was, and how clean, not unlike a corridor of a newly opened hotel. The walls were a soft yellow colour and there were small tables dotted alongside the wall. Cantered on each little table was an ornate vase which held a neatly organised selection of white or pink flowers.

There were various doors spaced evenly along the hall, and each had signs which read things such as 'STORAGE', 'STAIRS', 'DRESSING ROOMS', 'LOBBY' etc. James was looking for one sign in particular. Reaching the end of the hall James had to double back. Recognizing their voices James glanced around the corner and put faces to the two men he had heard earlier. They were just down the next corridor and approaching his position. Crouching, he quickly and quietly back-tracked up the hall keeping an eye over his shoulder. Just managing to get to where he began in time to see them turn the corner, James took the other hall and couldn't believe his luck. The second door down this hall just happened to be the one he was searching for. 'STAGE'. Without thinking he opened it and quickly entered, his main concern was getting out of range of detection of the two in the hall behind him. Breathing heavily he slumped against the door on the inside and looked up.

It was dark, and there was no chance he would be seen clearly in the shadows if there had been someone on that side of the door. James listened through the door he'd just entered and heard Silas and the other man joking as they passed. Once more he was reminded of how he was alone. Had he had someone by his side he could easily have handled that situation without having to flee. This whole thing was far from what he was used to, and it wasn't yet over. Mustering his confidence he made up his mind to continue. Leaving the door behind him he crept through the room keeping to the shadows, ahead he could see a small passage with lead to the stage-side. There were old wooden beams along the wall and overhead. The strong smell of cheap perfume, wet paint and old wood shavings filled his mind as he moved along. Creeping closer to the passage he began to hear the low hum of a roaring crowd somewhere not far off.

Reaching the passage he slunk against the wall and hid beside a thick beam of timber supporting the wall. Beyond the beam he could see two, perhaps three men manning the ropes and patrolling back-stage. There was one very muscularly built man standing in front of him right beside where he was concealed. He must have been around 6ft and had very broad shoulders. That ruled out trying to take him on face-to-face instantly. James glanced around for inspiration. 'Three minutes' James caught someone nearby say, and he began to panic, he was going to run out of time if he didn't pick up the pace. Looking up he could see there were some rather conveniently placed sandbags attached to some nearby ropes. James made a choice. Taking a deep breath he dove out from his hiding place past the tall man and kept going. He ran past the men and around behind a curtain to behind the stage.

Instant chaos broke out around him, the man shouted and the other two noticed James. Hopping over a beam on the ground he ran for the ropes. Loosening the right one, James glanced back, gauging the distance of his pursuers. When the time was right he let go and the bag fell, one man crumpled under the weight of it and white powder created a screen thick enough to slow down the other two. James took the moment and legged it around the back of the stage to get beside a blackout curtain. Just in time, the curtain was raised and the crowd was deafeningly loud, the audience was on their feet applauding and there were shrieks of excitement as the stage darkened and a spotlight shone on the centre. James looked on, waiting for her to step out on-stage... and then his throat caught, terror grabbed him and he froze. He was on the wrong side.

He had precious moments to get this done and he wasn't able to change his position now. Inside his mind was screaming, behind him he could hear the men were going to be on him any second. In a panic now he could see his target approaching the stage on the other side. Taking the small gun from his coat pocket he looked down and in that moment his photograph fell out onto the ground. Time stood still as he knelt and picked it up. His heartbeat was all he could hear now and his chest was heavy as he stared at the photo of his love. Glancing up he saw it was now or never as his target stepped out on stage. Taking in the beauty of the smiling girl on the photo he felt tears in his eyes and this throat felt tight as he kissed the photo and closed his eyes tightly. Pocketing the photo, reality hit him and noise returned, behind him more men were alert and were gaining on him.

Taking the deepest breath, James walked directly out onto the stage, arm outstretched and aimed at her temple. Meeting centre stage he pulled the trigger and shot her clean through her skull. In the same second the theatre erupted in commotion with screams of horror and alarm, he tried to make for the exit but had barely taken a step before he was grabbed and held down, the weight of two grown men keeping him in place. His gun was knocked from his hand and he struggled helplessly, glancing across the stage he could see people in tears and shrieks of agony at the realization of her death. He had at least succeeded. A sharp blow came then to the back of his head and his face hit the stage with a heavy thud as red came over his eyes and sensation began to fade. A deafening high-pitched ringing sounded through his mind as more impact came to the back of his head, he could taste blood.

He knew he wasn't going to survive this. The image of his now never-to-be fiancé's photo clouded his mind; he would never see her again. Within a second his sight disappeared, and he was left in blackness.

When the Past Bites Back

By Deniss Jerlikovs, aged 18.

It's been ten years since I nearly drowned him and I still remembered him! He stood no more than an arm's length from me, oblivious to the presence of his attempted murderer, oblivious to me. As one, the world seemed to cave in, the walls closed in on me, the cameras observed like grim watchers and the people around stared, judged and hated me for nearly ending a life I had no right to take. The past memories I fought to forget came screaming back at me, forcing me to see the boy drowning, forcing me to witness my own ecstatic delight in his suffering on that day.

I feel my mind lose control as I collapse to the floor, screaming and kicking wildly, trying to block out the terrified screams of the boy. A hand reaches for me, but I fight back, falling into the depths of my own mind, drowning just like him. The last I see is their faces, looking frightened, as all goes black.

* * *

I hate queues, and lines, and just waiting! People tell me that I should pace myself more, but that would bore me. I have been standing here, waiting in the bank for a simple lodgement, but the old man up front just HAD to ask about EVERYTHING! Like, seriously, who asks about coffee shops in a bank, of all places? People also told me that I should complain less but I just complained that complaining less would bore me some more which would lead to more complaining. That usually shuts them up!

The line finally slithered forward, kind of like an annoyed sloth. I liked the bank, it was quick business (obviously not today), painted blue and had a really high ceiling, often reminding me of swimming underwater. I recall my first experience of swimming, when I nearly swam like a rock about ten years ago. I think of the girl who pushed me into the pool, the same girl that made sure my life was hell at school.

Suddenly, like unexpected lightning, the woman in front of me collapsed into a fit of very loud screaming, shivering on the floor like it was ice cold, banging and convulsing wildly. I reached out my hand to help but she just kicked it and screamed some more. As suddenly as it began, she stopped screaming. I could see that she fell unconscious, judging from her death-like stillness.

The annoying old man blessed himself and muttered something about demons. People stood and stared at the woman like people stare at zoo animals. Me, I nursed my sore hand and wondered what had just happened. There was a very uncomfortable silence in the room, except for the clicking of the wall clock. I decided that calling an ambulance would be a good idea by now.

When the ambulance arrived, the paramedics came in. They loaded up the girl in one of those wheeled-bed-things and carted her away. One paramedic, a woman, did a double-take when she noticed me and, completely out of the ordinary, told me go with her to the hospital. I contemplated not giving a damn and just lodging my money, but the look she gave me told me that I needed to be a good boy and get in the vehicle. I'm twenty one, not five, by the way!

When I got to the hospital and the still unconscious woman was taken away somewhere, I was confronted by a doctor. 'That is the woman who nearly killed you. She is traumatised by that.' He stated this as if a person nearly dying is normal in a casual conversation. My brain jammed and I burst out laughing at how bluntly the doctor had said this. Imagine a person getting an iron bar, strapping multiple fish to it and hitting you repeatedly with it. It hurt a lot and smelled fishy.

Out of nowhere, a nurse shoved the doctor aside, glaring at him with eyes of little hell flames, at which he smiled smugly. 'I have told you countless times to stop creeping people out like that!' She fumed. I felt really out of place as the two bickered back and forth. I compared myself to a sixth finger, having no idea what to do or how it got there. Eventually, the hushed shouting match ended and the nurse told me to follow her.

As we walked, I thought about the doctor's words. 'So, she's the same girl that made my life miserable back then.' I recalled the insults, punches, kicks and general douchebaggery that she did to me. I felt my body grow heavy and my walk slow as my spirits darkened to these memories flashing in my eyes.

I barely noticed the nurse point down a corridor, telling me that I needed to take the left door. I turned as instructed, deep in my thoughts, and walked straight into the wall. Recoiling and clutching my nose in pain, I manoeuvred around the very offending wall.

Walking into the corridor, I could see a door to my left quite a bit away but the corridor seemed to stretch before my eyes, taunting me to walk. It was eerily quiet in the hallway with the only sound coming from my own footsteps. I increased my pace to the door, stared at her name on the door panel and slowly entered through the portal to my painful past.

I was confronted by the view of a peaceful sleeping woman, the same woman from the bank, the same girl from way back before. I noticed her squirming and watched her eyes slide open slowly, examining the surroundings and eventually falling on me. I don't really know what to say, so I went for an old classic;

'Lovely weather we're having, eh?'

* * *

I find myself drifting, like an uncertain boat bobbing on the tides of life. I think of the past and colour slowly seeps to life around me, creating a scene that forces me to catch my breath.

I stood in front of myself, my ten year younger self. The place was of that day, outside the local swimming centre, the same day and place when I tried to drown him. It seems as though time has been frozen here, the water won't move, the falling leaves from the trees won't move and the boy floating directly above water won't move...

Examining my young self, I see the glee and satisfaction on my face as I admire the sight of the drowning boy, whose hand is stretched out, begging for help. Despite the distance, I could feel him gripping at my soul, as though he wants to pull me down with him.

I turn, wanting to leave, but my past self stands in front of me, looking at me with a predator's eye and a sickly twisted smile. I scream and try to run but she grabs me, effortlessly tossing me into the pool. The surface of the pool shatters around me and I fall into a deep darkness.

I see phantoms around me, the faces of my parents, my family, and my friends. They screamed and roared out 'monster' and 'tyrant', 'murderer' and 'villain'. Over and over, the voices echoed and the faces moved closer, gaining on me, as though they were forcing me lower, banishing me away. I try to fight them off but my hands faze through, and I realize that this is my punishment, my suffering, my---

The world exploded and I could feel the cold embrace of sheets, could taste the strong scent of medicine in the air. I knew where I was but I didn't want to face the white walls, psychiatrists and stale food. I open my eyes to look around... only to see him standing by the door. Fear gripped my heart for the upcoming torment. He opened his mouth and I felt my soul cry in terror.

'Nice weather we're having, eh?'

113

It felt so surreal, I couldn't help but look outside at the weather; it was sunny, as sunny as his smile. I expected shouting, screaming, blaming but not this alien kindness. I didn't notice him sit by the bed until he spoke again.

'I've run out of my short cliché stockpile, so how about we get to know each other now?'

I stare at him, not recognizing him but at the same time totally recognizing him. I feel as though I am still asleep, not really seeing the real him.

* * *

'This is awkward,' I thought to myself, sitting near this obviously confused woman. There didn't seem to be anything I could say, unless...

'Y'know, I walked into a wall back there,' I say while pointing at my nose. 'Probably did a lot of damage too, to the wall that is!'

That somehow got rid of the tension a bit and she rewarded me with a small smile. I could see she was still nervous but she managed to speak, 'I, um, stubbed my toe on the doorframe...?'

I couldn't help but laugh at this, like Romeo and Juliet! Love at first sight that ends in pain and misery!' We both have a small laugh. The tension seemed to have melted some more now.

We begin talking about random things, like people do when they first meet. We talked, chatted, laughed and tried very hard to avoid the elephant in the room with the words 'DARK PAST' written on it. We eventually had to do something about the elephant, approaching the topic cautiously and carefully. It seemed to be difficult for us both but we managed and I saw she felt horribly guilty for having been a bully to me.

She asked me if I hated her and I truthfully told her that I didn't. 'Do you forgive me?' She asked next and I wasn't certain anymore. I thought if I did but was confronted by a darker thought, whispering sickly sweet evil into my mind. I grinned on the inside, 'I will forgive you if you do one thing for me…'

* * *

'Time to fly!' He shouts with joy over the wind and pushes me forward, off the tall building. I tumble and fall through the air, screaming and knowing that the ground was growing closer and closer every second. The wind slapped me across my clothes and face, burning it with cold passion.

I knew I was desperate if this was what I would do for his forgiveness. I knew it was foolish, dangerous but I would not rest peacefully without knowing the past was settled. It wouldn't last long now, with the street coming to greet me with frightening speed.

I could almost make out the detail of the cars and the people below me as they stared up at me. It didn't matter though, I was flying for my redemption. The ground seemed so close until…

* * *

'Time to fly!' I yell as I throw her off the building. I sadistically laugh as I hear her screaming down the length of the building. Peering over the edge, I watch her body, and her screams, grow smaller. This seemed like the perfect punishment in my mind and I felt satisfied enough to forgive her during her flight down. Where I swam like a rock, she is now flying like a rock.

I felt quite good at what I did, despite how evil it may be. Poking back over the edge, I see a small dot below me. 'Any moment now… Any moment…' Suddenly, there is a loud snap as it all connects…

And the bungee rope springs back, pulling with it a screaming bundle into the air. I fall over in a fit of laughter, holding my sides from the pains and knowing that karma will probably punish me for that little act but it was worth it. I also knew that she would be quite annoyed with me in the future for convincing her of jumping off a building, but that was for later. For now, I wanted to laugh heartily and let her bob on the rope for a bit. I forgave her.

A Tattered Coat

By Richard Maher, aged 15.

The springs in the king-sized mahogany bed shuddered and squeaked as Brian McGrath, aged sixty-three rose.

The sound of three separate clans of mice running for cover could be distinctly heard as Brian crossed the dust covered floor.

Their footprints were as clear as their droppings in the corners. Brian reached the hallway and walked down the moth eaten carpet. Brian had a weather-beaten face; his nose appeared to be squashed from all the gales it had faced.

He had matted, dirty, grey hair and bushy eyebrows. When he smiled, Brian's electric blue eyes would shimmer, then his teeth would become apparent; most blackened; but others were a distinct shade of yellow.

Brian pulled on a faded blue Aran jumper – oh, how it had kept him warm, his worn-out jeans and an old tattered coat. Brian's wife Valerie had bought it for him, back in the day.

It had once been a beautiful beige; now however, it is a nondescript, grimy grey with a pungent odour of sheep nuts and noromectin pour-on. The coat had seven pockets, containing a few unknown keys, some soggy dog biscuits, an unidentified ball of wire, some squashed Rolos and an old, barely functioning Nokia mobile phone.

As Brian left home he glanced at a cobweb-infused picture of his family. Brian, not being one for sentimentality, shuffled quickly on. As always, worry lay heavily on Brian's mind. Brian creaked the lop-sided door closed behind him. Milly, Brian's great companion ran attentively to him. Milly was a beautiful fourteen-year-old sheepdog. She had a black face, with beautiful white and brindle patches, and eyes full of kindness. Together, as always, the two companions trudged up the farm passage and started another day's work.

The battle-hardened duo passed all the run-down sheds, the dilapidated parlour, ducks waddled and splashed noisily around them as they passed the pond. Still, they kept walking up a steep incline. Brian wheezed, he had lost the fitness of his youth. They reached the gate to the 'Top Field'. Milly ran off to herd the sheep. As Brian's breath returned and his wheezing subsided, he took stock of his surroundings and allowed his mind to wander. Brian lived on the mountain of Carrantuohill, the tallest peak in Ireland, the McGraths had lived and farmed there for centuries. It was Brian's fortieth year at the helm. When his family were young, Brian had bought land, reclaimed mountain and was a highly respected farmer. Now Brian was a lonely, tired old man who missed his family dearly.

Milly had brought the sheep to Brian. His beloved Scottish Blackface ewes – tough, hardy survivors, much like Brian. There had been twins born during the night. The first lambs of the year. They were twin ewe lambs, the future of the flock. They bounced around happily. The mother had been bottle-fed by Brian's son. Brian remembered how he had loved the animals. The ewe was looking decidedly pleased with herself. Brian fished a Rolo out of one pocket and gave it to the ewe. Brian chuckled, even after all the years, seeing the new lambs still brought sheer delight to Brian and the shadow of a tear to his eye.

As Milly and Brian made the somewhat easier descent home, he heard the ringtone of his old Nokia. The noise muffled by the coat pocket. Brian quickly retrieved the phone. It was his son, Tim. Brian's heart swelled with happiness. He gingerly pressed the little green button.

'Hello' said Brian, trying to contain his excitement.

Brian waited for an answer; it didn't arrive. Brian glanced at the screen. No signal. Typical. Brian sighed and with a heavy heart he hung up.

The sky was full of menacing grey clouds, rain began to pelt from the heavens, raindrops the size of golf balls. Brian and Milly picked up their pace. When they reached home they were soaked to the skin.

Brian put his tattered old coat over the Aga and heated a tin of beans. The best before date was four years ago, but it was common knowledge that tins held forever. Valerie had taught him that much. Brian sat at the drooping table and surveyed the grotty kitchen. Damp infested the walls, the paint was peeling, appliances were defunct and doors hung off shelves. Brian exhaled sharply and promptly began eating his beans out of the saucepan. Brian left half for Milly, who gobbled them up. Of course they didn't have dinner the night before. At nine o'clock, Brian realised nobody was going to call. He made the solitary journey to his bedroom.

He didn't wake up.

Three days later Tim and Gloria walked up the cobbled path to the back door. Tim was the image of his father but less wrinkled, Gloria was a tall, thin, pretty woman with dazzling green eyes. A wedding ring glistened on her finger. Tim hugged Milly; she remembered him well. It was his first time home in over seven years. Tim absent-mindedly imagined the surprise his father would get. If only he'd answered the phone he could have gone to the wedding, the old codger. This was the next best thing, however, he surmised.

Or so he thought, Tim opened the door and called his father. There was no reply. Gloria checked the sitting room, still no sign of Brian. Maybe he was on the farm? No, Milly would be with him. Tim checked the bedroom. His father lay still and at peace, the constant wrinkles vanished from his face.

It wasn't the homecoming Tim anticipated.

At the funeral, the common consensus was that Brian was with Valerie, and that was a blessing. Brian was once again happy. For Brian's children, Tim, Rose and Breda, grief was all-encompassing. But as with all bereavements, soon after the dust settled and life returned to normal.

Well, Tim and Gloria didn't leave the small family farm on Mount Carrantuohill. They didn't return to their high-flying jobs. They swapped suits for wellingtons, nights at restaurants for nights in the lambing shed and swapped meetings for the mart. Tim didn't want his family's legacy and all his father's hard work to go to waste. The house was renovated, the farmyard modernised, children were born, ewes lambed and Milly had puppies.

The only thing that didn't change was that every morning, Tim would pull on his fathers tattered old coat, a grimy grey with seventeen pockets, still smelling Brian's aroma and sensing Brian's spirit. Guiding and protecting him.

POETRY

The Insult

By Johnjoe B. Gurry, aged 14.

Today, at school,

I was insulted.

This insult was sharp as a blade,

Piercing as a cry,

Raucous like a laugh

And soft as silk.

It was strong as a man,

Weak as a fly

Which takes off and shudders when touched.

Carrying as a voice,

Troubling as grief,

Black as night

Bright as the sun

That covers me today in golden rays,

This insult fragrant as a rose,

Venomous as a snake, sly as a fox

And deep as the sea, so calm, so blue.

I dare not repeat it, lest you feel

All these emotions,

And it touches you as it touched me.

Sanctuary

By Joseph Cheetham, aged 14.

Last time I climbed a tree
I kinda fell and hurt myself,
But I got back up and climbed it again
To build a tree house so I could play
Video games in peace away from my family.
I made a rope ladder to get up easily.
I ran extension leads from my house
And brought a mattress up to sleep on;
My parents couldn't find me for two days.

Our Separate Paths

By Sam O'Carroll, aged 16.

I stand here today to say my thanks
For all the memories we've made,
But as they came those memories
Will slowly start to fade.

We'll finish school, go to college,
Find jobs and start to date,
Get married, raise kids or a whole other bunch of things.
For these memories it'll have been too late.

We'll have lives to live and families to love
And all new memories to make.
We'll make mistakes and regret a lot
And have all new fears to shake.

But then we'll scour our Facebooks
Or find some old photographs.
Those memories will flood our minds once more
Our fears, our cries, our laughs.

For one day our time will come
And our ghosts cast into oblivion
Our lives on Earth may be no more,
But our legacies will live on.

So, goodbye, dear friends, I've had a blast
And hopefully you have too.
I'll take my leave down my separate path
Till we meet again, Thank you.

See you on the other side…

Broken Friendships

By Saoirse Duignan, aged 14.

Movement happening all around me,
Murmurs surrounding me,
How did this happen to me?

Old friendships,
Fights,
What's the antidote,
For broken friendships?

Talking?
Listening?
I'm open to suggestions.

How do you heal a heart,
One that can't trust anymore,
One that is about to burst?

A Big, Fat Wonder

By Ellen McCarthy, aged 18.

Walking home late at night
Gazing at the stars,
How they shine so bright.
A big, fat wonder, it is tonight

Watching the night sky,
Catching every soul's sight,
The reflection bouncing off my eye,
A big fat wonder, it is tonight.

It goes past science, astronomy -
It goes past every living discovery.
Great minds have asked,
'What goes past that great big light?'
But it's all just a big, fat wonder
That ponders through life.

A Coma of Purple

By Arthur Finlay, aged 14.

A woman is wrapped in a cocoon of silk.

She dives into a nocturnal realm where nightmares creep into her mind and dreams float above.

A small orb of pale light appears in the darkness.

Her white dress flows around her frail frame.

She follows the orb on a journey far and wide, through willows that sway like broken spider webs in the wind, over hills that are covered in fuchsia flora where small plump fawns skip and play.

The stars shine bright in the Byzantium sky,

Delicate purple butterflies flit back and forth in front of her,

Black birds circle the moon.

Days pass, months and finally years.

A shimmering utopia fades as her journey comes to an end.

She sees a woman laid on her back, white dress, frail body, violet orchids in her raven-black hair, her eyes misty white, lifeless.

Her own body laid to rest as her soul carries on.

Felling Fire

By Emma Donohoe, aged 16.

The blade glinted fiercely in the shadows,

His breath, hot and ragged, battled against the frost.

Moss floated mournfully on the breeze

Around the gaping wound of pale, ringed wood.

Flickering fish of burning scales

Glide through the embers.

Timber groans drowned by flames

Of hissing heat.

The Wind

By Cathy Keaney, aged 17.

The wind is a wonderful thing.

It can knock you down,

Or take your breath away.

It can make your heart beat fast

And your hair dance.

It can blow away the paper cups

And make you run and laugh,

Or cry and shiver.

But most of all it makes you feel your fingertips

And the way you either fall

Or fly.

The Argosy

By Emma Donohoe, aged 16.

The angered cry of men
Was deafened by the roar of the sea,
And the waves swelled like a wild beast against the hull.
Sails were hastily clawed down,
And oars pulled back, but to no avail.
The cloth was torn,
Wood splintered,
And the muscles of men strained under soaked shirts.

Sorceress had left the port to the cries of the foolhardy,
Women embraced, and heads of children, tousled fondly,
As the boys went to play sailors.

All were oblivious to the sunset;
Dying before their eyes, tainted,
A threatening crimson, deeper than their blood
Running in streams down sweat-soaked backs.

Regret had grown to bitter resentment
Of each man and wave and cloud.
They hung above with an irritable air of late warnings.
Foam and fear slopped over the deck,
And the murky deep churned ferociously
To the stormy symphony clashing through the skies.

Phantoms howled through the minds of men,
Causing eyes to roll and tongues to rave
Of the living horror that slowly dragged them down.
Shadows draped over weary lungs and sails alike,
Drowning the bodies and boards.

All the while, dawn approached,
Bringing forth fabled hope and light;
Only to turn sour upon wretched sight.
Insides of the vessel littered the glassy surface,
Not unlike confetti that had sent the Argosy on its way
before.

The dawn shone on till word reached home,
And women fell on their knees and wept
As the skies' tears fell bitterly on the ruin
And the scars left behind.

Silence fell, muffling the sounds of struggle,
Beneath the swirling darkness.
Lungs burned fiercely and muscles screamed,
As air escaped in a flurry of bubbling clouds.

Pale strands and streams of light,
Tentatively reached into the depths;
Illuminating the sinking fortunes.
Priceless jewels floated within grasp,
Worthless trinkets in His eyes.

He passed bargained crowns and bloodstained gems,
To carefully collect the fallen.
He comforted their still hearts,
Softening expressions of torment,
To those of eternal slumber.
Each soul crowded toward Him;
Like eager children awaiting play.
Their voices echoed weakly,
Last thoughts of terror, anguish and regret...

He thought it dreary.

Every being slipping by,
Without the slightest tug of rare strength.

But what was this?
As He held out His hand,
To beckon yet another into his embrace,
Defiance was surely shown in swift kicks toward the surface.
His cloak curled around this exception's face,
And, for a moment,
The sun shone on pale, glazed eyes...
Before courage fought back anew with might,
Bringing forth a burning desire to live!

The surface was in reach, the rippling bright taunting
Penetrating cold stiffened thoughts and limbs.
The light glared and sharply blinded,

As the surface broke and lungs greedily gulped air;
Sweet, sweet air!
The salty tang of the sea,
The warmth of life and sunshine.

Frantic flailing brought refuge from Him;
Scrambling onto a fragment of sodden deck,
Shivers shook the man's exhausted frame with angry force.
Attempting to comprehend, desperate for a sign
Gazing searchingly up above, like thousands before him.

This man lay gasping upon wreckage,
Unaware that He was watching
He stood with crowds of countless souls,
Feeling cheated out of the best of them.

www.ingramcontent.com/pod-product-compliance
Lightning Source LLC
Chambersburg PA
CBHW060124260626
47160CB00005B/2012